ADE ADEPITAN

CYBORG CAT

AND THE
MASKED MARAUDER

This edition published in Great Britain in 2020 by
Piccadilly Press
The Plaza, 535 King's Road, London SW10 0SZ

www.piccadillypress.co.uk

A CIP catalogue record for this book is available from the
British Library.

ISBN: 978-1-848-12850-7

1 3 5 7 9 10 8 6 4 2

Typeset in OpenDyslexia-Alta by Perfect Bound Ltd

Printed and bound by Clays Ltd, Elcograf S.p.A.

MIX
Paper from
responsible sources
FSC® C018072

Piccadilly Press is an imprint of Bonnier Books
www.bonnierbooks.co.uk

CYBORG CAT

AND THE
MASKED MARAUDER

Ade Adepitan
illustrations by Carl Pearce

Piccadilly
PRESS

1

A Very Rude Awakening

THE zombies were closing in. There must have been at least a thousand of them and the sound of their low, anguished moans followed me.

"Stay calm," I said to myself but, as I turned the corner to find myself faced by a wall, a dead end, I knew that really wasn't going to be easy.

I had to act, and act fast.

I took a deep breath and focused.

A moment later I felt a familiar surge of energy from my chair. We were one, pulsating and humming with power.

Suddenly, I took off. I free-wheeled straight up to the top of the wall in the chair, then somersaulted backwards. I came down onto the heads of the approaching zombies and proceeded to bounce off them, splattering them one by one, as if I was in some sort of horrific pinball machine...

BANG! BANG! BANG! BANG!
RING! RING! RING! RIIIIINNNNNGGGG!

I opened my eyes groggily. Was this part of the dream?

BANG! BANG! BANG! BANG!
RING! RING! RING! RIIIIINNNNNGGGG!

No, there were no zombies anywhere. I wasn't in my wheelchair, and I definitely wasn't dreaming. In fact, I was wide awake and tucked up in bed.

"Aaaah! Aaaah! Who is banging on our door at this time on a Sunday morning?!" I heard Dad shout as he hurried down the stairs. "This had better be important."

My dad was born in place called Ogun State in south-western Nigeria. Mum says the locals there are like the Bristolians of Nigeria because they have very strong accents. When Dad was angry or concerned his Ogun State accent became super strong.

I strained to hear what was happening as Dad opened the door.

"Aaah, Brian! Have you won the lottery? Is that why you are banging on our door like a madman?

"Erm, well, actually, no... Well, yes, but ... erm, could I see Ade, please, Mr Adepitan?"

Dad must have said yes because the next thing I knew Brian came bounding up the stairs and into my room.

"If you have won the lottery," Dad shouted

after Brian, "tell your father I would like a new Ferrari, and maybe a year's supply of moi moi! That should be enough to compensate for waking me up so early."

"Hi, Bri—" I started to say. But before I could even finish saying his name...

"It's gone. All of it! Gone! Vanished! Stolen! Every last penny! I put it —"

"Whoa, Brian, stop. Take a deep breath. What are you talking about?"

Brian blinked. It was almost as if I'd pressed pause on a remote control. He'd been talking in fast-forward and now he was completely still. Then, a moment later, it was like I'd pressed play, but at normal speed.

"Last night, after we'd

finished the car wash, I went home with the money we'd raised, thirty-six pounds and seventeen pee, and put it in the strongbox in the shed, like usual, with the rest of the money we've collected. And then I locked the strongbox. I definitely, definitely locked it. Definitely."

"Okay, Brian, so then what happened?"

"Nothing."

"What do you mean, nothing?"

"Well, then I just went to bed and fell asleep."

"Brian," I said, as calmly as I could, "I don't mean what happened the moment after you locked the strongbox. What happened that made you come round here, trying to smash the door down at eight in the morning?"

"Oh, I see," he said. "Well, this morning I got up and went to check the strongbox and that's when I made my terrible discovery. All the money, all one hundred and eighty-six pounds and forty-nine pee, has gone!"

"What?!" I shouted, now wider than wide awake. "How can that be possible?"

"Well," said Brian, "I've given that a lot of thought and got it down to three possibilities. It could have been eaten by a hedgehog that used one of its spikes to open the box. Aliens who can pass through solid material might have taken it. Or it could have been stolen by someone who has the key."

"I think it might be that last possibility, Brian," I said. "But I thought you had the only key?"

"So did I," he said. "But my mum says that make of strongbox uses the same key for all its boxes, which might explain why we got it for half price from the pound shop."

"All the money!" I exclaimed, as the news began to sink in. "All the money! This is terrible."

"Erm, yes," said Brian. "But there's something else."

"What?" I felt like a punchbag that had just had all the air whacked out of it.

"It might be best if you see for yourself, Ade."

"Yeah, the money's definitely gone, no question about that."

"Dexter," I said. "I don't think Brian asked us all to come round here just to confirm that the money has gone. *That* is what he wanted us to see."

It was about fifteen minutes since Brian had nearly bashed my front door down and the Parsons Road Gang had gathered at the scene of the crime.

The 'something else' Brian wanted us to see was lying on the ground next to the open, and – as Dexter had correctly pointed out – empty strongbox.

"It's a clown mask," said Shed, stating the obvious.

"Well done, Sherlock Holmes," joked Melody, but no one was really in the mood for jokes.

"There's a folded piece of paper underneath it with your name on, Ade," said Brian. "I saw it when I lifted the mask up with my dad's spade."

"Why did you lift it up with a spade?" enquired Salim, asking the question that was on all our minds.

"Fingerprints, of course," said Brian. "This is a crime scene. Whoever stole the money has probably left their fingerprints all over the mask and that evidence will be a vital clue when it comes to solving this crime."

"What about the person in the shop they bought it from?" said Shed. "Their fingerprints will be on it too."

"Yeah," said Melody. "And anyone else who picked it up to look at it in the shop, but decided not to buy it. That could be loads of people."

"Yeah, Brian," said Dexter. "But I have worked something out from the clues."

"What's that then?" Brian asked.

"You're a silly sausage and an even sillier detective who couldn't work out what day it is if you were looking at a calendar."

"So what day is it then?" I said, jumping to Brian's defence.

"Erm, well, it... I think... That's not important right now," spluttered Dexter. We all chuckled, but then quickly got serious again as Shed bent down and picked up the mask. Sure enough, underneath it there was a note for me.

My name had been written in green crayon. It looked as if a three-year-old had

done it. As I stared at the big, chunky letters
I could sense my wheelchair thrumming
and my Cyborg Cat powers kicking in. The
message I was being given was clear: this is
not good.

"Go on," said Dexter impatiently. "Read
it."

I picked up the note and, with five pairs of
very wide eyes expectantly watching me, I

opened it. The same green crayon had been used to write inside it in weird letters of varying shapes and sizes. But it was what it said that really chilled me to the bone.

Forget about playing 4 Newham Rollers. Your not needed and your not good enuff. You'll never be a barsketball playa, back off now or else!!!

Underneath the message, this time in red crayon, was a signature.

The masked marauder

My chair was pulsing with energy. I looked over to the clown mask that Shed had picked up. I could hear it laughing madly at me, taunting me, challenging me.

Hahahahahahaha haaaaaaaaaaaaa!

Suddenly, the mask grew in size until it was touching the ceiling. As it towered over me, the empty eyes of the mask bore into my head and I began to feel dizzy and sick. My temples throbbed. I turned away quickly as a single drop of cold sweat trickled down my back.

There was no doubt about it.

I had a new nemesis.

2
A Big Match and a Missed Catch

Three weeks earlier...

"HANDBALL!"

"Dex," I said. "We're playing basketball, remember. You're allowed to use your hands in basketball."

"Oh yeah, sorry, I forgot," said Dexter. "It's just that in my head I keep commentating on the game as if it's the Cup Final."

"Must be the strangest Cup Final ever,"

Brian said. "How have you been ignoring the fact no one's kicking the ball?"

"Everything's strange in Dexter's head," chipped in Melody.

"Come on," Shed shouted. "Let's get back to the game. How about me and Ade take on the rest of you this time?"

Two against four. I liked the sound of that. It would be a real test of my new skills in a wheelchair, not to mention my new powers, which I'd felt growing ever since tackling that tarantula on the school trip to the safari park.

"I've got a better idea," said Salim. "Me and Ade against the rest of you. Wheels against the good old-fashioned two-leggers. What do you think?"

I *really* liked the sound of that. It wouldn't be easy, though, mainly because I was back in my really-not-very-sporty-at-all hospital wheelchair.

After the safari park trip, the headteacher had spoken to my parents and told them she was happy for me to come to school in a wheelchair. Dad had reluctantly agreed, but he still found it hard to accept. He couldn't quite let go of his Nigerian attitude that people in wheelchairs were at a big disadvantage and would struggle to get anywhere in life. However, he was adamant that he wouldn't let me use Salim's spare chair.

"We've never accepted charity, Doyin," he'd said. "And we're certainly not going to start now."

So I was lumbered with a heavy, brown, difficult-to-manoeuvre chair. It was nowhere near as mobile and cool as Salim's, but I'd been practising all the tricks he'd taught me and I was getting more and more confident every day. And, of course, I also had my Cyborg Cat powers.

"That's silly. You'll have no chance," said Shed.

That settled it.

"Wheels against two-leggers it is then," I hollered, getting as close as I could to Shed and then swinging round to wheel behind him, before reappearing next to Salim. "Let's do this."

"Yeah," said Salim. "Bring. It. On."

We bumped the bars on the front of our chairs together. There was a metallic thud as they hit. Salim and I smiled. It was our way of doing a high-five. Then we turned and faced up to the other four.

"Game on," said Melody. "Dexter, just remember it's basketball not football. Use your hands, okay?"

"Yeah, don't worry, the Cup Final in my head's just finished," said Dexter. "West Ham beat Spurs fourteen–nil. I scored a quadruple hat-trick."

"Like that's ever going to happen," said Shed, a little sourly.

"Come on," I said excitedly. "We'll even let you start."

I threw the ball to Brian, who just about caught it, and the game began.

Brian passed to Melody, who moved forward and to her right, bouncing the ball. As I went across to block her run, she passed to Dexter, who took the ball in his stride and tried to jink inside Salim, who was marking him.

Salim was quick, though, and stayed tight to Dexter, who looked up and saw Shed standing unmarked. Dexter threw the ball to him and ran forward, hoping for a return pass, but the ball flew past Shed and out into touch.

"She-ed!" shouted Melody, Dexter and Brian together.

"What?"

"You didn't even try to catch Dexter's pass," said Brian.

"Yeah, and it was probably the greatest pass in the history of basketball, even a butter-fingered zombie could've caught it," added Dexter.

"Sorry, I was miles away," Shed apologised, looking sheepish.

"Don't tell me you were playing a Cup Final in your head too!" said a somewhat exasperated Brian.

"Something like that."

"Come on," said Melody. "Get your head in the game; we need you."

"Yeah, yeah," said Shed, his eyes suddenly

lighting up. "Don't worry. I got this, guys. I'm back, hundred per cent. Now let's crush these two losers!"

Shed wasn't joking. He played out of his skin for the rest of the game. He was their side's top scorer by far, but Salim was in a different league to the rest of us. He played regularly for the Newham Rollers Under Fifteens, a local wheelchair basketball team, and his experience and skill helped us to win 48–36.

It was a good laugh, and by the end we were all drenched in sweat and gasping for something to drink.

"Come on, Dex," shouted Brian as Dexter attempted to drink an Olympic swimming pool-sized amount of water from the water fountain in the park. "Leave some for the rest of us."

"O – GLUG – KAY – I'M NEARLY – GLUG – FINISHED."

A few minutes later we'd all quenched our thirst and started heading out of the park.

"You know, Ade," said Salim. "You've got some skills on the court. I've never seen anybody move so well. It's like you've got a natural connection with your chair. Normally it takes years to get that good."

I shrugged, slightly embarrassed by Salim's compliments. My chair made a low humming noise that only I seemed to notice. I'd discovered that the Cyborg Cat energy inside me could be transferred to whatever chair I was using. It felt good, but I knew I was only scratching the surface of my powers. I couldn't control them yet – sometimes they were there, and sometimes just gone.

"He's good at everything," said Shed. "He's the Cyborg Cat."

"Yeah, and Cyborg Cat's powers are limitless," chipped in Dexter.

"I don't know about that," I said. "I'm not sure I could take on an alien Tyrannosaurus rex with super strength and the ability to read minds."

"Of course you could," said Melody. "Especially with us backing you up. A mind-reading T-rex wouldn't stand a chance against..."

She cupped her hands together, making her voice boom out loudly around us.

"... the incredible, the mighty, the unstoppable Parsons Road Gang!"

"Yeah!" we chorused, high-fiving and whooping and hollering like we'd won the FA Cup and the NBA Championships at the same time.

"I'm serious, though," said Salim. "You should try out for our team. Coach Carlos is looking for new players in the Under Fourteens – I reckon you'd get in easily."

"Yeah, you'd walk it," said Brian. "Er, if you see what I mean."

"I don't know," I said. "Dad's still not very happy about the wheelchair. He's worried people will make fun of me."

Brian scratched his chin.

"Well, if you came to school in your wheelchair wearing that crazy pink suit again then that would be a source of great hilarity," he mused, agreeing with himself and nodding vigorously.

"Yeah, that pink suit was jokes." Dexter chuckled, remembering the colourful outfit my mum had insisted I wear for my first day at Credon Road School.

"Ade, this is a great chance to show your dad what you can do," said Salim.

"Yeah," Melody agreed. "I bet he'll be pretty happy about what people think when you're being crowned player of the season."

"But what if I'm being crowned worst player of the season?" I said, suddenly unsure about my skills.

"I don't think there's a crown for being the worst player of the season," said Brian.

"There might be," said Dexter. "But it'd be shaped like a dustbin lid. Or a big curly poo."

We all laughed at the thought of that.

"What do you think, Shed?" I asked, turning round.

Shed seemed to be lost in his own thoughts again. His dad had lost his job a few weeks ago and even though no one actually said anything about it, we all knew it was making things difficult for Shed's family. He was one of my very best mates, though, and I wanted to hear his opinion.

"What?" he said, distracted. "Oh, yeah. The basketball team. Weeelll ... I, erm, I think it could be a good idea."

"That's great," I said.

"Oooorrrr," he went on, "it could be a bad idea."

"Thanks, Shed," I said. "You've been a great help."

"Come on, Ade." Salim wasn't going to

take no for an answer. "I know you're good and I'm the best judge in the world. When your dad sees you scoring basket after basket he'll change his mind, I'm sure of it. So what do you say?"

I stopped for a moment and shut my eyes, searching for my Cyborg powers. As I put my hands on the wheels of the chair energy coursed through my body. A moment later I felt a gentle but familiar surge as my chair radiated in harmony with me.

I opened my eyes.

"Let's go for it!"

PARSONS ROAD E13

BOROUGH OF NEWHAM

3

Trial by Mum and Dad

I STARED at the calendar on my bedroom wall.

I'd circled Saturday 4th May and written **5 p.m.** inside it. The trial was still over a week away, but I could feel that day pulling me towards it.

It was as if I was moving through a long tunnel, getting nearer and nearer, but before I could reach the light, there were some twists and turns to deal with. I hadn't told Mum and Dad about the trial yet, but I figured that when I did it would be best if things were going well at school and at home. So I had to take a detour into some side tunnels marked 'homework' and 'washing up' from time to time, but my main focus was still the trial.

I'd been meeting up with Salim as often as possible for basketball practice. He was a great teacher. The rest of the gang had improved as well, and Dexter had even started calling Salim "Professor Basketball".

Dexter didn't always take it too seriously, though. One day he turned up with a set of giant foam hands with pointy fingers. He reckoned the big hands would give him an advantage. We had to laugh. He had no chance of catching, dribbling or even holding the ball with them on.

In contrast, Salim was always super-focused. He concentrated mainly on me, and

I'd come on leaps and bounds.

"I know you're right-handed, but try to dribble the ball with your left hand," he told me. "That way you won't be predictable. Remember, let the chair do the work. You only need one or two pushes and even your chair will roll forever."

I did as he said and sailed past Brian into clear space. Salim looked pleased.

"Okay, if this was a real game," he continued, "I'd want you to keep your head up, look to pass to someone in a better position, then cut to open space and –"

I interrupted before Salim could finish.

"Yeah, but it's not a real game," I said cheekily. "So instead, I'm going to do this."

I glanced up quickly, raised the ball into a shooting action and let it go. I was a long way from the basket but it arced through the air and...

SWISH!

That was the beautiful sound the ball made as it splashed through the hoop without touching the sides. The net seemed to flutter with satisfaction as if it approved of my shot.

"Woo-hoo!" shrieked Melody. "That shot had added Cyborg Cat power, Ade."

"I know," I said. "I think I even surprised myself with that one." My heart was pumping like mad; it felt like the beginning of something great.

"You're going to blow them away at the trial, Ade," said Brian.

"Well, I don't know about that," I replied modestly.

The truth was, I was feeling more and more confident about my basketball ability. I loved playing and even though the others said my Cyborg Cat superpowers were helping me, I wasn't so sure. Out on the court it just felt natural having a ball in my

hands and dribbling and shooting.
It didn't feel like when I became
Cyborg Cat; somehow it just
felt like me.

"Are Shed and Dexter coming
or shall we just play a quick two-on-
two?" asked Salim.

"Nah, they won't be here," Brian told him.
"Dex said he had an England football match
to finish off in his head and Shed said he had
to go straight home after school."

"So me and Ade against you and Salim
then?" Melody suggested.

"Fine with me," I said. "But shouldn't you
be doing more football training to prepare
for your trial?"

"Yeah, Melody," said Brian. "Basketball
isn't going to help you get onto the school
football team, is it?"

"Actually, it could do," corrected Salim.
"It's good fitness training, and some of the

skills, like pass and move, are much the same. Plus, there's the mental alertness. You have to stay switched on the whole time in basketball, just like football."

"Thanks, Professor Football," said Melody, grinning. "Don't worry, Brian, I'm doing plenty of football training, and anyway, I've got my lucky boots. I've scored every penalty I've ever taken with them on. I'm not worried about the trial. I'm going to be the first girl on the football team, you'll see. Let's play!"

For the next ten minutes we played a fast and frantic two-on-two game. No one could really keep score, but I sank a good few baskets, so I was feeling pretty positive.

"You know, if Dad comes home from work in a good mood tonight, I'm going to tell him and Mum about the trial," I said.

"Go for it," Salim said.

"Yeah, and maybe do this at the same time!" Brian had picked up the basketball and was attempting to spin it really fast on one finger. Unfortunately, it lasted about a second before falling off and rolling into the bushes.

We all laughed.

"Great idea," said Melody. "That'll really impress Ade's mum and dad."

A moment later, the ball came rolling back out of the bushes. We waited for someone or something to emerge after it. Nothing appeared.

My Cyborg Cat senses kicked in: something was strange. I had a definite feeling that someone had been there, even though, when we checked, the bushes were empty.

Weird. I shook the feeling off as we headed home.

• • •

"Here you go, Adedoyin," Mum said. "Amala."
She smiled and put a plate of delicious-
looking food in front of me. Amala means
"pounded yam" in Yoruba, the Nigerian
language she speaks. She poured a gooey,
rich, spicy okra stew on top of it. My
stomach rumbled. It was one of my favourite
meals.

"Wow, thanks, Mum,"
I said, eager to devour
every last morsel.

"This is good brain food,
Doyin," she said. "It must
be why you're doing so well
at school."

I beamed when she said
that and a huge grin caterpillared across my
face as I scooped up my first spoonful.

"I'm home!"

It was Dad. I instantly replayed his 'I'm

home' in my head. It was upbeat, and he didn't sound too tired. Sometimes if he'd had a bad day he could barely force the words out and they sounded heavy and distant. This sounded like a good 'I'm home'.

Of course, I didn't pounce straight away. I let Dad sit down and have a cup of tea. He and Mum chatted about their days, and then Dad asked me about mine.

I told him about a project we were doing in geography and getting one of the top marks in a maths test. Then I went for it.

"So, erm, Dad," I said. "You know I've been playing a lot of basketball with my friends?"

"Have you now, Doyin?" said Dad. "Did I ever tell you about the time I was crowned Wastepaper Basketball Champion at work? I got fourteen baskets in a row and –"

"Ah, ah, Bola," interrupted Mum. "You've told us a million times."

"Yes, Dad," I said. "And it's a great story,

but what I wanted to tell you was that Salim thinks I'm a really good player and –"

"Of course you are," said Dad, smiling. "It must be in the genes."

"Only if there's a gene for throwing scrunched-up bits of paper into a rubbish bin," Mum said, laughing.

Dad laughed too. They were both definitely in a really good mood. I ploughed on.

"Well, the thing is, Salim plays for a team called the Newham Rollers and they're looking for new players. He thinks I could get in and there's a trial, so I'm going to go along and –"

"What?"

Dad's 'what?' landed with a big thump in the middle of my sentence. This wasn't good.

I took a big gulp of air. I suddenly felt really nervous and a jolt from my chair went right through me. I sensed I'd made a big mistake. Something was badly wrong.

My brain said, "Stop now, Ade. Quick, change the subject," but there was nothing I could do – my mouth just kept moving.

"Next Saturday," I went on. "That's when the trial is. Of course, I might not get in, but if I play well I think I've got a good chance."

The atmosphere in the room had changed. It was as if a dark cloud had moved across the light. My powers seemed to be flickering jerkily, as if they were trying to connect, but something was stopping them.

"No, Doyin," said Dad sternly. "I do not think it is a good idea. It is one thing to mess about with your friends but playing wheelchair basketball for a team is something completely different."

"But, Dad, I really think I –"

"I said no, Doyin. It is bad enough that people stare at you in the street, but there isn't anything we can do about that. This is just asking for trouble, showing off in front of people. Anyway, it will be a distraction from your schoolwork. The only way you will get a good job and do something with your life is if you do well at school. There is no future in basketball."

I wanted to say something, but all the energy had drained from my body. My Cyborg Cat powers were totally gone. There was just nothing there. Would there ever be again?

Dad hadn't ever liked me being in a wheelchair but I'd thought he was getting used to it and that he might see possibilities rather than limitations.

I was wrong.

I looked at Mum, willing her to speak up

for me. I was sure she'd understand how important this was to me.

I was very wrong.

"Listen to your father, Doyin," said Mum. "This basketball thing is just a silly dream, like it was with football. It is foolish. Your studies are the most important thing. You must keep working hard and maybe one day you will get a good job as a lawyer or a doctor."

CREDON
ROAD   E13

BOROUGH OF NEWHAM

4

I Spell Trouble

"ADE? Ade? Ade!"

"Eh? What? Where am I?"

Then I remembered. I was at school.

"Oh, sorry, Mr Hurst, I ... erm ... is the answer twenty-seven?"

"Well," said Mr Hurst, "the question was, How do you spell the word 'introduction', so what do you think?"

"I ... think it's not right," I said, feeling embarrassment rise up through my body.

"Course it's not right, you idiot!" I knew

that was Spencer, but I couldn't even be bothered to react to him. Most of the class was sniggering.

"That's quite enough, thank you, Spencer," said Mr Hurst. "Ade, you've been doing very well in class lately, so I'm going to let this small lapse pass, but do please try to concentrate."

"Yes, sir," I said.

I managed to get through the rest of the lesson without incident, but I was pretty relieved when the bell went for break.

"The bell is for me, not for you," said Mr Hurst as we all started to get up. "Please sit down again."

"But sir, it's play time," came a voice from the back of the classroom that sounded suspiciously like Dexter.

"This will only take a minute," said Mr Hurst. "Mrs Bolton has asked me to remind you about the whole school assembly at the end of term. Mr Jenkins is planning what I've been told is a fascinating science talk, but other contributions are welcome, so if you have any ideas, sign up on the noticeboard. There, that wasn't too long was it? Off you go."

"What shall we play?" Dexter asked me excitedly as we got into the lift.

Since I'd started using a wheelchair, school had made some adaptations to help me, and installed a small lift over the summer holidays. There was just room for me and one other person. There had been so many arguments about who should come with me in it that eventually Brian had drawn up a rota. It was colour-coded and had taken him an entire weekend, but it actually worked well.

"I don't know," I said dejectedly. "I don't really feel like playing anything."

"But it's Play Time," said Dexter. "We have

to play at Play Time, otherwise they might stop calling it Play Time, and then we'd have to do whatever they decide to call it, and it might be Eating Worms Time or Smelling Feet Time."

I smiled weakly, but even Dexter could tell something was up.

As the doors opened the others were waiting.

"You're it," said Melody, tagging me and running away.

I wheeled out of the lift slowly.

"Come on, Ade," said Shed. "Try to catch us."

"Yeah," said Brian. "You should know how to play tag by now – we've played it every day for the past two years."

"And this is a really good way to stay fit for your trial," shouted Melody, who was now quite a long way away.

"There isn't going to be any trial," I said, the words tumbling out of my mouth like rocks.

"What?" said Dexter. "Have they cancelled it?"

"Does Salim know?" asked Brian.

"No, I don't mean there isn't going to be a trial at all," I explained. "I just mean there isn't going to be a trial for me. I'm not doing it."

My friends reacted as if I'd just fired a freeze-ray gun. They all stopped moving and stood completely still with their mouths wide open.

Melody was the first to crack.

"Wh-why?" she stuttered.

"Because it's a waste of time," I snapped. "I watched some of the team play yesterday

and they're brilliant. I haven't got a chance
of getting in, so I'm not going to bother
trying. I'd just look stupid."

That wasn't true, of course. I was too
embarrassed to tell my friends the real
reason I wasn't going for the trial. Apart
from anything else, if I did go for it and get
onto the team, when Mum and Dad found

out they would be so angry I'd gone against their wishes that they would stop me playing anyway, so it was pointless.

Brian was the next to defrost.

"But, Ade," he said, "Salim thinks you're good enough, and he should know!"

"Yeah," said Dexter. "And you've got superpowers as well and we'll all be there to support you because we're the Parson's Road Gang and we always stick together."

I knew my friends were disappointed. They'd been looking forward to watching me play and cheering me on if I got onto the team, but the way I felt that was another reason not to do the trial. If I didn't get through they'd all be gutted and I didn't want that responsibility.

I was about to change the subject when Shed suddenly thawed out.

"You're exactly right, Dex," he said. "We always stick together. If Ade doesn't want to do the trial, we should support him and not try to change his mind."

It was like Shed had fired his own freeze-ray gun. I was stunned. I'd expected them all to try to convince me to go for it. Especially Shed, who was always on my side.

"Erm, yeah, thanks, Shed," I said eventually, a little unsure about what I really felt. I mean, I guess he was being on my side. But I wasn't sure I liked it.

"But Cyborg Cat can do anything, Shed," said Brian. "Ade could get on to the team, I know he could if he wanted to."

"But he doesn't want to, does he?" retorted Shed.

They all looked at me. I knew I was expected to say no I don't, but my stomach felt as if it had thousands of ants crawling around inside it. I just felt confused.

"Hey, loser, spell introduction – ha ha ha ha ha!"

For once, I was almost happy to see Spencer and his mates.

"Get lost, Spencer!" I shouted.

"Yeah, you couldn't even spell it, anyway," snapped Melody.

"I know it's not spelled twenty-seven, though, ha ha ha ha ha!"

"That's because you probably think it's 1,396," Dexter shot back.

Spencer looked at Dexter oddly – we all secretly did – then shrugged his shoulders and went to walk away. He suddenly turned round to face us again.

"Oh yeah," he said, "good luck with your trial, Melody. You're going to need it."

"What did he mean by that?" I asked Melody as we watched Spencer walking off.

"He doesn't want a girl on the football team," she said. "Spencer and his mates have been trying really hard to make me look bad at practice. They almost never pass to me, and when they do they hit the ball so hard I can't control it."

"Probably because they know you're brilliant and ten times better than all of them put together," blurted out Brian, immediately turning a little red.

"Ten times? I'd say a hundred times," said Melody, shaking off her concerns. "You're it!"

She tagged Brian and we all headed away from him as fast as we could. The weird mood was broken.

It felt good to be playing together again, but I knew the confusion about me not taking part in the trial hadn't completely gone away.

Had I made the right decision?

5
The Best of Friendlies

"WHERE are we going? I can't see a thing."

It was Sunday morning and I was blindfolded. Melody and Dexter were taking me to a mystery location.

"You're not going to wheel me onto that roundabout in the middle of the North Circular and leave me there, are you?"

"Actually, that wasn't the plan," Dexter said. "And just so you know, this part of the plan was all my idea. Brilliant, eh?"

"Yes," I replied, baffled. "Totally brilliant, you are a genius."

"I know," Dexter went on. "But that roundabout idea sounds great. We could call it EXTREME WHEELCHAIR NINJA WARRIOR."

"What?!" Wearing the blindfold, I couldn't tell if he was being serious or not.

"You silly sausage!" Melody chuckled. "Of course we wouldn't do that, Ade."

"Phew," I responded. "Well, then, maybe you're going to take me to a space rocket and send me to the moon?"

"Believe me," said Melody. "If we could do that, I'd be the one going myself. Don't worry, we're nearly there and then you can take off the blindfold."

I tried using my Cyborg Cat powers to figure out where we were going, but nothing happened. Either there was no danger ahead or my powers still hadn't returned. I very much hoped it was the former. I used my ordinary senses instead, but that turned out to be a mistake when we turned a corner and my sense of smell told me that a lot of dogs had been using the area for a toilet.

Five minutes later we stopped.

"Okay, Ade, we're here," Melody announced.

"Where's here?"

"Here!" said a different voice as the blindfold was whipped off me.

I blinked as light hit my eyes. I was on the basketball court in the park and in front of me were Shed, Brian and Salim.

"What are we doing here?"

"Spectating," said Brian.

"Yeah," said Dexter. "The Newham Rollers Under Fourteens are going to be here in a minute for a practice match. Salim's refereeing and we thought you might like to watch."

"But we also thought you might not like to watch," added Brian.

"Okay," I said, confused. "Why? You're not going to get me to do some cheerleading or anything like that are you?"

"Course not," said Salim. "The others told me that you weren't going to do the trial, and they thought you'd gone off basketball for good. So Dexter came up with the idea of the blindfold. He thought if you knew where you were coming to, you might not have come."

"Well, actually," interrupted Brian. "What Dex said was, you might dig a huge hole in your garden and go and hide in it, and end up liking it so much, you'd live in there forever."

"Yes," said Dexter, beaming. "I did think you would come out for supper and to go to the toilet, though. And to go and watch West Ham if you had a ticket."

"Anyway," said Salim. "I know you still

love basketball, so there's no reason not to watch a game, is there?"

"Yeah, and I'll make sure you get home in time for lunch after," said Shed. "And you don't even have to wear the blindfold again when we leave."

"Thank goodness for that," I said. "When are the players getting here?"

"Right about now," said Salim.

Sure enough, a few moments later the team arrived and started warming up.

"Whoa!" I gasped, totally mesmerised as the Rollers made their way confidently onto the court, wearing slick red-and-white vests.

I'd never seen so many people in wheelchairs in one place before. They looked so cool. I loved the way their chairs moved effortlessly across the court, and how they all looked like superhuman athletes, their arms so big and muscular. I couldn't imagine anyone laughing at these

guys. A warm glow flowed through me and,
as I watched the players stretching and
taking a few shots, I felt my chair hum a
little, as if it was enjoying watching as much
as I was. Were my powers starting to come
back?

"They do look good, Ade," said Melody,
who was standing next to me.

"Really good," Shed agreed, nodding. "I

think you definitely made the right decision not to do the trial."

"No chance!" shouted Dexter. "Ade could run rings round this lot, couldn't you, Ade?"

I didn't reply. I just kept looking at the players warming up. They really did look good, but something told me I wouldn't have been out of place playing with them.

I shook the thought out of my head. I was just there to watch.

By now the players were getting into position for the opening tip-off. I could only count four players on one of the sides – there should be five on a team.

"Where's Tommy?" I heard Salim ask.

"Dunno," said one of the players. "He said he was going to be here."

"Well, he isn't, so you'll have to play four against four until he arrives," said Salim.

"What about your mate?"

I looked round for Salim's mate but I

couldn't see anyone. When I turned back everyone was staring at me.

They meant me!

"What about it, Ade?" asked Salim.

"Eh?" I said. "But what if Tommy turns up?"

"Yeah," said Shed. "I'm sure he'll be here any minute."

"Well, then you can go back to spectating from the sidelines," Salim replied. "Just help us out while we wait for him."

"Go on, Ade," said Brian. "It's just a training game."

I could feel excitement surging from me to the chair – or maybe it was from the chair to me. I didn't want to just watch. I wanted to play. But I was still hesitant.

"Would you like to borrow my giant foam hands?" Dexter said. "I can run home and get them."

There was no need to answer that.

I thought about what Cyborg Cat would do and felt my chair respond. It pulsated mischievously beneath me, urging me to move forward. That was good enough for me.

"Just until Tommy shows up, right?"

"Of course," Salim said. "Just till Tommy gets here. Now come on, and don't forget what I taught you."

I didn't need to be asked again. As my friends cheered, I raced out onto the court and introduced myself to the other players.

"Tommy's rapid," said a player called Wesley. "He scores lots of points for us on fast breaks and usually defends the quickest guy on the other team. That'll be your job today, though it might be difficult in that chair. Are you ready for this, rookie?"

As he spoke my chair jerked forward, forcing me into Wesley's footplate and nudging him backwards.

"What are you doing? Calm down," I mumbled, hoping nobody would notice I was speaking to my chair.

Wesley gave me a bemused look.

"No problem," I said, loudly, taking up my position.

I could feel the adrenaline pumping through my body. It was mix of excitement and nerves.

"Relax," I told myself. "It's just a bit of fun."

My chair didn't seem to know that, though. Its wheels were powering up and beginning to glow. I could feel energy surging into my body. Fun or not, I was determined to show everyone just what I could do.

Peeeeep!

Salim blew the whistle and we were off.

I took it easy at first, even though I could feel the energy from my chair pulsing. I prowled around the court like a hungry tiger. Then, with a couple of quick pushes, I managed to lose my defender.

"Over here, I'm open!"

Wesley rocketed a pass in my direction. The ball flew towards my chest like a bullet and I felt a charge of Cyborg Cat energy shoot through me as I caught it.

Quickly placing the ball on my lap I pushed down hard on my wheels and set off towards the basket. I weaved between two defenders, bouncing the ball before putting it back on my lap again.

Using all the strength in my arms, I pulled back on both wheels, forcing my chair to stop abruptly. One of the defenders saw this as his opportunity and lunged for the ball.

"Gotcha!" I whispered under my breath.

In one swift movement I flipped the ball into my left hand, just like Salim had taught me, leaving the defender grabbing at thin air. I had a clear lane to the basket now, but the player I'd just beaten wasn't giving up that easily – he clearly didn't want to be humiliated by a rookie.

CRAACKK!

I felt a sharp jolt as he rammed into the side of my chair. A spark flew up as his push rim hit mine, leaving the air smelling like fire. Somehow I kept my concentration and shot the ball in the direction of the basket.

SWIISSSH!

The ball flew through the net just as the defender and I tumbled into a crumpled heap of arms and wheelchairs a couple of metres away from the hoop.

"What a shot!" Wesley yelled.

The boy who'd been defending me gave me a fist bump and look of respect as we both got back into our chairs.

"Wooo-hoooo! Go, Cyborg Cat!" shouted Dexter as the others all clapped and cheered.

"Well played," said Salim as the game restarted.

After that basket, my confidence grew and grew. By half time I'd got another six and my team decided that the tactics for the second half should be 'get the ball to Ade as much as possible'.

I was buzzing. Our game had clearly turned into something of a spectacle, as quite a few passers-by had stopped to watch from the sidelines.

When the second half started I was straight into the thick of the action. My chair was changing colour as pulses of energy fizzed through it and into me. I was really enjoying myself.

If only Dad could see me, I thought, hearing the gang cheering. *Maybe he'd change his mind and realise that this is the sport for me.*

With five minutes remaining we were well

 ahead, but as I raced forward to collect a long pass one of the wheels on the front of my chair jammed into a pothole on the side of the court.

Before I knew it I was catapulted into the air. The strapping across my lap and my knees held me in the chair, but it didn't stop me from doing a couple of spectacular rolls along the floor.

Wesley and the rest of team started whooping and hollering. My acrobatic tumble had impressed them. Thankfully, apart from feeling a little embarrassed, I was fine.

"Now, that was a proper wipe-out!" Wesley shouted from across the court.

Well, at least they think I'm cool, I thought, lying on the ground and chuckling to myself.

"Are you all right, Ade?"

It was Shed. He'd come racing over as

soon as he'd seen what had happened.

"You gotta be tough if you wanna be a serious baller, rookie," another player said as he rolled past me, smiling.

"I'll help you up," Shed said, offering an outstretched hand.

"No need, mate, I'm fine," I said, heaving myself up before shouting to everyone else, "Come on, let's get on with the game!"

I charged back to my position as Shed retreated to the sidelines.

A little while later it was all over and my team had won convincingly 56–38.

As I shook hands with the other players, there was plenty of back-slapping and compliments on how well I'd played.

"That was amazing," said Melody, as my friends gathered round.

"Yeah," said Brian. "You were easily the MVP."

"M V what?" said Dexter.

"Most valuable player," Brian replied. "That's what they say in basketball. It's like Man of the Match in football."

"Yeah, you played well, Ade," said Shed. "But it was only a friendly. Shall we head off?"

"Nah, not yet. I'm still buzzing and I want to talk through my performance with the prof," I told him.

"Fine," said Shed. "Then I'll see you at school tomorrow. I've got to get home."

"See you," I said. "Erm, say hi to your mum and dad from me."

Shed didn't respond as he headed off. I'd wanted to say something about his situation at home and that's what came out. I felt foolish and a bit awkward, so I quickly shook the feeling off.

"Hey," I said, wheeling over to Salim. "Lucky for me that Tommy didn't turn up, wasn't it?"

"I don't think Tommy had much chance of

making it from Dublin," Salim said casually.

"Eh?" I was baffled. "What do you mean?"

"Tommy's in Dublin this weekend with his family. He won't be back till this evening."

"But I thought he was meant to be playing," I said, confused.

"And that is indeed what you were meant to think," said Brian.

"Yeah," Melody explained, "because we knew you'd only play if you thought that you were helping make up the numbers."

I was confused.

"But why was it important that I played?"

"Because," said Salim, "there's someone who wanted to see if you were really as good as I said you were." Salim pointed to a tall man with dark hair standing on the sidelines. "Carlos our head coach is over there by the bags. And he'd like to have a word with you."

6
Measuring Up

"SO, you're the famous Ade?" said Carlos, offering me his hand to shake. As we'd wheeled over, Salim had told me that the coach had once played professional basketball in Spain.

"Erm, I'm Ade, yes," I said nervously. "But I'm not famous."

"You wouldn't know it the way Salim goes on about you." Carlos laughed. "He talks about how good you are all the time."

I didn't know who was more embarrassed,

me or Salim. I mean, I knew Salim rated me, but I had no idea he'd been telling his coach about me.

Thankfully, Carlos continued before things became too awkward.

"And you know, from what I've just seen, I think Salim might be right."

"Really? Wow. I mean, thank you. I, er ... well, I'm pretty new to the game and I know have a lot to learn, but I love it. It just feels great playing."

"Good," said Carlos. "Then I'll see you here for training on Tuesday evening."

"What?"

"Seven o'clock. Don't be late. You played really well in that chair, but it's not right. It's way too big and the footplate is too low. That's probably why you took a tumble earlier. The league won't allow you to play in that; it's dangerous. We'll get you measured up for a sports chair."

"Are ... are you offering me a place in the team?" I spluttered.

"Well, in the squad, yes. From what I've seen this morning, you're definitely good enough. So, what do you say?"

I looked at my friends, who were looking at me with wide-eyed expectation.

I really, really wanted to say yes – but what would Mum and Dad say when they found out? Now that I knew I was good enough, if they stopped me from playing I might never forgive them.

As I felt the conflict raging inside me, instinctively I shut my eyes and put my hands on the chair. Its energy instantly entered me.

I was Cyborg Cat and I could do anything.

"Yes," I blurted out. "Yes! I'll be there."

"Boom! The Parsons Road Gang do it again!" cheered my friends, jumping around with excitement.

I looked at them and shook my head. They'd planned the whole thing. They knew Tommy was away. They also knew that I wouldn't be able to resist playing when asked to fill in for him, and they knew Carlos was going to be there.

"Thanks," I said to them. "But that's the last time you lot blindfold me and take me anywhere! I thought you were going to wheel me to a rubbish dump and leave me."

We headed home, laughing about all the places Melody could have taken me when I'd been blindfolded – the giraffe enclosure at the zoo (Brian's suggestion), a cell at the police station (Salim's idea) and the pocket of a giant who loved toffees and kept a big sticky bag of them in there (Dexter's idea, of course, which got the biggest laughs). At home, after a much-needed shower, I felt exhausted, but at the same time really excited. I couldn't wait for the training session on Tuesday. Fine, I didn't quite know how I was going to deal with my parents, but I felt more determined than ever to show them what I could achieve. It wasn't going to be easy, but I wanted them to know that playing wheelchair basketball was not going to hold me back.

Monday and Tuesday at school seemed to go on forever. I kept wishing time would speed up, but it didn't listen to me and plodded along like a miserable donkey with a bad leg. The weather didn't help either. It rained both days, which meant wet play. At one point I thought Dexter might actually explode if he didn't go outside and run around. Brian tried to cheer us up by inventing a football quiz, but Melody and Shed got into an argument about one of the answers, and Shed went off in a huff on Monday lunchtime that he still hadn't shaken off on Tuesday.

After school I told Mum and Dad that
I was going to hang out with the gang in
the park, so they weren't surprised when
the doorbell went. Dexter and Brian were
standing on the doorstep.

"I know Melody's at football training,
but where's Shed?" I asked in surprise. "I
thought he was coming. He hasn't gone to
live in a big hole in his garden, has he?"

Dexter chuckled.

"No," said Brian. "He said he couldn't
come cos his auntie was coming for tea."

I knew we were all thinking the same
thing: Shed was still in a huff.

When we arrived at the park Carlos called
me over.

"Good to see you, Ade," he said. "Right,
five times round the outside of the court as
fast as you can. Go!"

"He doesn't mess about," Wesley said,
wheeling up beside me. "Chat comes later.

We get straight down to it. That's why we're one of the best teams around."

I didn't mind that. If I was going to be the best, I'd need to play for the best – after all, it was a team game.

After another ten minutes of fitness training, we split into groups of three for a sort of piggy in the middle game, where one person had to get the ball off the other two, who weren't allowed to hold onto it for more than two seconds.

It was tough. I was really sweating at the end and mightily relieved when Carlos said we could have a short break. I started to head over to Brian and Dexter, when a voice stopped me.

"Don't think you'll be getting my place in the team so easily again, mate," it said.

I immediately got a bad feeling. My chair wheels glowed an angry, dark red.

I turned round to see a broad-shouldered

…oy with green eyes, glaring at me.

"Lucky for you I was in Dublin," he said. "Otherwise there's no way you'd be here."

"You must be Tommy," I said.

"That's me," he replied, bringing his wheelchair right up to me so that we were practically eyeballing each other. "I'm the power forward on this team, and don't you forget it."

"I —" I started to say, but he'd gone without waiting for me to speak.

Part of me wanted to go after him, because I didn't like the idea of any of my new teammates having a problem with me, but obviously Tommy wasn't in the mood to sort things out right at that moment.

I felt certain Tommy and I would be able to sort it out and become friends in the future. I understood where he was coming from. A new player coming in meant more competition for places. That could be a good thing and a bad thing – makes you try harder, but there's a greater chance of not making the team.

The rest of training was great. Carlos pushed us hard, but the advice he gave was fantastic and I found that little adjustments to my game could make a big difference.

"You did well, Ade," Carlos said when we'd finished. "How did you find it?"

"Awesome!" I exclaimed. "I can't wait for the next one. Or to play in a real match. If I get picked, of course."

"Well, this is still pre-season training at the moment," said Carlos. "The first match isn't for a while yet, but that's a good thing. You've got talent, Ade, but there's a lot to work on if you want to improve. And it'll give you a chance to get used to your new sports chair. *Vamos!* Let's get you measured up."

I'd learnt from Salim that occasionally, without thinking, Carlos would drop a

Spanish word into a sentence, especially when he got fired up about something. *Vamos* with the 'v' pronounced like a 'b' meant 'come on' or 'let's go!' The team affectionately called it Spanglish.

Sport with language lessons thrown in, I thought. *How could Mum and Dad not love that?*

Carlos and Jordan, one of the other coaches, started taking all sorts of measurements. It felt weird having a tape measure being run up and down all over me, but there were so many things that needed to be taken into consideration: the seat and backrest width, the backrest height, something about the degree of wheel camber, which turned out to be the angle of the wheel in relation to the ground. Apparently, if I got that right, it would help me turn my chair much more quickly, which is perfect for beating defenders one on one.

They also talked about footrest position and lots of other technical stuff. Listening to Jordan and Carlos made me feel like my brain had been fitted with one of those camber things itself, and my head was spinning at a hundred miles an hour.

"The basketball wheelchair is a technological piece of art," said Jordan, with a mystical look in his eyes. "Get one measurement wrong and it will totally ruin your game."

Jordan had played for Great Britain when he was younger, so he knew what he was talking about. I gulped. This was serious.

It was exciting, though. I'd done pretty well in my standard-issue hospital chair and that definitely didn't feel as if it was because of my Cyborg Cat powers. They were there when I played, of course, but it felt more as if they were cheering me on than helping me. My achievements on the basketball court so far had all been down to hard work and, though it felt a little big-headed to think it, natural talent. The thought of a new sports wheelchair filled me with excitement. I was sure I would reach incredible new heights in it.

But then I was hit with a bombshell. A massive one.

"Okay, that's everything we need," said Carlos. "If we put the order in soon, we could

get your new chair just before our first game of the season. We'll need the £250 deposit first, though. You can pay the remaining £500 once it's been delivered."

"What?" I blurted. "That's ... that's..."

My mind went blank. All I knew was that it was a lot of money. An awful lot of money.

"Seven hundred and fifty pounds," said Brian helpfully.

"I thought the club provided the chairs! I haven't got that sort of money," I said helplessly.

"I'm sure you don't," said Carlos, smiling. "Just let your parents know – they can send the deposit to me."

Without realising it Carlos had just lit the fuse that would lead to a massive explosion.

"Can't I borrow someone else's chair?" I pleaded. "Or what about if I keep playing in this one?"

"That chair isn't legal," said Jordan. "The

British Basketball League have got a lot stricter with the rules this year and, even with adjustments, it just wouldn't cut it."

"If you want to maximise your potential," added Carlos, "and compete with the best players in our league, you need to have a chair designed and built to your body shape. Using someone else's chair won't do."

"Right," I said, unable to keep the disappointment out of my voice.

I explained the situation with Mum and Dad to Carlos and Jordan, but they said there wasn't anything they could do. The club just didn't have enough money to buy chairs.

"We have to pay the home court referees, table officials and court hire fees for training," said Jordan. "And food and transport for the away team on game days."

"After all that," said Carlos, "there's very little left."

Carlos could see I was distressed. He

looked sad but he put his hand on my shoulder to try to comfort me.

"Lo *siento*, Ade," he said.

I looked at him confused.

"I'm sorry, Ade," he translated. "But you can't play without a chair."

I looked at the Rollers' players cracking jokes and mucking around. All of them had custom-made basketball chairs. Their chairs looked super cool, but somehow I just hadn't thought that I'd need a new chair too. Now I'd found out that they were so expensive, my dreams of becoming a superstar basketball player looked like they were over.

For good.

7
Sponsored by the Parsons Road Gang

"I'VE got sixteen pee and three buttons," said Dexter, as we made our way back to Parsons Road.

"Thanks, Dex," I muttered. "But –"

"Oh, hang on a minute!" he said excitedly, rummaging in his pocket. "Four buttons!"

"Dexter," said Brian. "Ade needs seven hundred and fifty pounds. After your sixteen pee he'll still need seven hundred and forty-nine pounds and eighty-four pence."

"What about the buttons?"

"Oh yeah, I forgot about them," said Brian. "If we include the buttons, Ade still needs seven hundred and forty-nine pounds and eighty-four pence, but you need a new shirt."

"I can't believe it," I said. "I'm sure the England football players don't have to pay for their own kit."

"No," said Brian. "But this is a wheelchair basketball team in East London, Ade. It's a bit different."

"I know, but ... I suppose I just assumed..."

My voice trailed off. I was gutted, of course, but I also felt stupid for thinking the chairs would be provided. In fact, I just hadn't thought about it at all.

"You know, when the youth club my brother goes to wanted a table tennis table, a load of them did a sponsored trampolining session," said Dexter. "They trampolined non-stop for eight hours, raised a hundred million pounds or something, which I think was enough to buy two tables."

"I don't think it would have cost quite that mu—" I started to say, but before I could finish my sentence, a strange sort of yelp came out of Brian's mouth.

"Yeek! That's it! Dexter, you've done it again. You're a genius. Ade, that's what we're going to do!"

"Where will we get a trampoline?" asked Dexter.

"Dex, for a genius, you can be a very silly sausage," said Brian. "It doesn't have to be trampolining. We can do loads of other things to get the money – sponsored walks, swims, bike rides, anything. What do you think, Ade?"

"I ... I ... I..."

"You ... you ... you..." they mimicked.

"I don't know," I said eventually. "Do you think it'll work?"

"Course it will," said Dexter. "With the Parsons Road Gang on the case, you'll have your super-cool basketball wheelchair in no time at all."

"Okay, then I think it's a great idea!"

"Yes!" shouted Brian, punching the air. "Let's tell the others and we can have a planning meeting after school tomorrow."

At four o'clock the following afternoon we were all sitting in Brian's front room. He had a clipboard and a notepad and was treating it like a very important business meeting, even though his mum had laid out crisps and lemonade, and we all had to be home for tea by six, which I don't think is what happens in real business meetings.

"Right," said Brian. "You know the plan, let's hear your ideas."

The Parsons Road Gang were brilliant: they had loads of suggestions. Along with Brian's original ideas of a sponsored walk, swim and bike ride, we also came up with a sponsored headstand, silence, car wash, juggle (even though none of us could juggle), dance, sleep (ruled out for being too easy), hoopla, press-up-athon, sing-song, doughnut-eating and a sponsored donkey ride at the beach (as long as someone could take us to a beach where they had donkey rides).

Those were just the sponsorship ideas. Salim suggested a cake sale, because his sister had done one and made loads of money. Dexter came up with the best – and the worst – idea. He suggested we should have a twenty-four-hour fart-athon. He even came up with a catchphrase.

"Give us your pence for flatulence," he announced confidently.

The room went silent as we all gave Dex a look that said, "Are you serious?" before we fell about laughing.

Brian was the first to recover and got us back to our senses by slamming his hand on the table (although he did spill a lot of lemonade in the process).

"Right, then," he said, mopping up with a tissue. "I've made a note of all those ideas and you will all be receiving a copy of them for your own records."

"What records?" said Shed.

"Yeah, my dad's got lots of records, but I haven't got any," added Dexter.

"I don't think Brian meant those sort of records," I said. "Or did you, Brian?"

"No, I meant – oh, it doesn't matter. Let's decide what to do first."

"Hang on a minute," Melody cut in. "I've got another idea. How about asking Emily to make posters?"

"Emily? Emily the graffiti artist? Emily aka the Night Spider who tried to scare Ade off the safari park trip and then released a tarantula when we were there?" Shed said.

"Yes," said Melody.

"She doesn't like Ade," Salim pointed out.

"Didn't like Ade," corrected Melody. "I've been talking to her at school and she's really sorry about what happened. I reckon this would be her chance to prove it to us."

"I don't know," said Shed.

"I think it's a great idea," I said, cutting in. "In a strange way, if she hadn't done what she did, the school wouldn't have seen how good I am in a wheelchair and I wouldn't be here now, trying to raise money for a sports one."

"Yeah, but can we trust her?" Shed said.

My chair suddenly glowed and vibrated a little, giving me the answer.

"I'm pretty sure we can trust her," I told them. "Plus, Emily's a really good artist and I bet her posters will help us a lot. We all know how powerful they can be. Go for it, Melody."

"So," said Brian, "what shall we do first?"

After a lot of discussion it came down to two ideas: a sponsored doughnut-eating contest or a sponsored press-up-athon.

Dexter was disappointed that we didn't consider his fart-athon, but he was very keen on the doughnut idea and said his mum could make a hundred doughnuts easily.

Melody preferred the press-ups, because eating doughnuts wasn't exactly the best preparation for her football trial and because, as she pointed out, Dexter hadn't actually asked his mum to make the doughnuts, so she might not agree to do it.

Then Brian said that none of us were sure how many press-ups we could actually do, but that he'd seen someone on television doing forty in a minute.

"I could beat that easily," shouted Dexter, who had forgotten about the doughnuts for the time being.

"Go on then," challenged Shed.

"Okay, watch this."

A minute later an exhausted Dexter rolled over, barely able to speak.

"How ... how ... many ... d-d-did I do?"

"I think I counted seven," said Brian. "But it might have been three."

We all fell about laughing. Seeing Dexter struggling was so funny that we decided we had to see it again. A sponsored press-up-athon for the Parsons Road Gang it was.

I headed home feeling pretty positive. Even if we didn't raise enough money for my sports wheelchair, we were going to have a good time trying.

8
Press-Up Pressure

"A SPONSORED press-up-athon! That is the stupidest thing I have ever heard. Whoever came up with that must have only half a brain."

"Actually, Spencer," I said, "we came up with it."

He turned round to see me, Melody, Emily and Dexter staring daggers at him.

"What a surprise," he said. "I suppose you're raising money to get the other half of a brain to share between you?"

"Well," countered Melody, "if you'd bothered to read the rest of Emily's poster, you'd see exactly why we're raising money."

"Why would I bother doing that?" sneered Spencer. "It would be a waste of time. Just like you trying to get into the football team. See you later, losers!"

Emily's poster was fantastic. It was a starburst of colours around someone doing press-ups, someone who looked a lot like me. She'd had a lot of practice drawing me, of course, back when she'd been tagging

PARSONS ROAD GANG PRESENTS

PRESS-UP-ATHON

Raising money for Ade's specialist wheelchair
Come and cheer us on!
MONDAY at 4pm, CREDON ROAD SCHOOL GYM

her graffiti the Night Spider, but at least this time it wasn't meant to scare me away.

"The poster's great, Emily," I said. "Loads of people are talking about it."

"Thanks," she said meekly. For someone who had once threatened to destroy me, she was actually quite shy. "But try not to look at it too closely."

"Wh-what do you mean?"

My stomach started to churn with nerves as I remembered the strange effect her graffiti had had on me, as if I was being pulled into it and a different world.

"Only kidding! Don't worry this poster's fine," she said, giving me a cheeky grin as she walked off, spray cans poking out of the pockets of her backpack.

This poster. Had she known the effect the posters had had on me? No. I felt certain that it was just my imagination. Emily was on our side now.

The press-up-athon was scheduled to take place the following day after school. We'd decided that instead of trying to do as many press-ups as we could at the same time, we'd take it in turns in a relay and keep going as long as possible. I was going to start, then, when I ran out of steam, Dexter would take over and so on. By the time it came back round to my turn, hopefully I should have recovered enough to go again. Our aim was to keep it going for three hours.

The others had already been sponsored by their parents and as many relatives as they could contact, but I couldn't ask Mum and Dad in case they found out what we were raising the money for. That meant I'd had to work a bit harder for help. Glenn at the market had been brilliant. He'd sponsored us and he'd got quite a few of the other stallholders to chip in as well, so I felt I'd done my bit. Some of the teachers and older kids at school had also agreed, though others hadn't been quite so friendly when we'd asked.

"Right," I said. "We've done well, but let's try really hard to get as many people to sponsor us as we can today, then all we have to do tomorrow is keep it up for a few hours."

"I'm going to ask the lollipop lady," said Dexter. "She always smiles at me, so I'm sure she'll say yes."

"She smiles at everyone, Dex," laughed Melody. "I think it's part of her job."

"Nah, she definitely likes me, you'll see."

As it turned out, the lollipop lady agreed to sponsor us thirty pence an hour, and said she would round it up to a pound if we completed three hours, which was not too bad, though whether or not that meant she especially liked Dexter was unclear.

We all agreed to practise doing press-ups in our bedrooms that evening, as we had done all week, and I made it to two and a half minutes easily. There were a lot of minutes in three hours, admittedly, but I went to bed feeling good. I knew it was going to be difficult, but my arms are pretty strong and the pressure on my legs wasn't going to be too great, so I reckoned I'd be able to manage.

The next day flew past and by four o'clock we gathered in the school gym, confident of achieving our goal.

Quite a few people had come along to watch. Brian's older brother Colin was the official timekeeper and checker (or 'adjudicator', as Brian later informed me was the proper title).

"Okay," said Salim. "When the person doing press-ups can't do any more, they have to say 'bogey' – that was Melody's idea – and then the next person has to start as quickly as they can. If they don't start, it's a fail. Got it?"

"Got it," we said in unison.

"Ade, you're up first," said Salim.

Shed helped me out of my wheelchair and I lay on a mat, ready to start.

"Okay," said Colin, ready to click his stopwatch. "Three, two, one, go!"

I pushed my hands down into the mat, lifted up with my arms and we were off. We'd already talked about the pace. If we went really fast, we'd probably burn out pretty quickly, so I took it nice and steady. I also knew, thanks to Brian's research, that on average people our age should be able to do between forty and fifty press-ups, so that was what I was aiming for.

It wasn't too bad at first, but as I got to thirty-five my arms began to ache and then the ache turned into a burn. I pushed up for one last time.

"Bogey!"

Brian was in position next to me and began doing his press ups. I rolled over, sweat dripping down my back and lay there, breathing heavily.

Thankfully, by the time Brian, Melody, Salim, Dexter and Shed had finished, I had recovered and was good to go again.

The first hour went well, but the second hour was a lot tougher. None of us could last as long as we had at the beginning, which meant we had less time to recover, and had to do more sessions each so it became a real slog.

That was nothing compared to the third hour, though. The pain in my arms was intense, and each individual press-up seemed like a huge, huge challenge.

The crowd watching us had thinned out, but those that remained were being really encouraging. By the last five minutes of the hour we were on our last legs – or arms, to be more exact.

Shed was in position, but he was really struggling. Dexter was meant to be next, but I could see there was no way he could go again, he was absolutely done for. Melody had had it as well and Brian had only just stopped and was practically passed out.

Even though I'd only had a short break, and even though my limbs were in agony, I knew if we were going to make it to three hours, I would have to jump in when Shed couldn't go on any longer. We were not going to fail.

"Cyborg Cat," I said to myself as I shut my eyes, "I really, really need your powers now."

Nothing. Just my body screaming in pain.

Okay, then, I thought – *if I'm not Cyborg Cat I'll just have to do it as Ade.* I wasn't giving up now. I looked at my hospital wheelchair. Yes, I *really* needed that sports chair.

As I looked at my chair, my whole body began to tingle. The chair started to radiate energy. Suddenly, a burst of light flew out of the wheel rims and up to the ceiling. It bounced back down and into my body.

My Cyborg Cat powers had found me. It was as if my determination to succeed as just Ade, with or without them, had summoned them. I felt the effect immediately.

"B-b-bogey," spluttered Shed, collapsing. Dexter was in position but struggling to push up.

"Three minutes remaining," Colin said.

"It's okay, Dex," I said. "I've got this." He rolled over gratefully, groaning.

I knew it was going to be tough, but I was not going to fail. I had to do it. I would do it. I was Cyborg Cat.

I pushed up – and almost collapsed immediately.

"Focus," I told myself. I concentrated on the energy-burst from the chair, feeling it run down my arms and along my back.

The extra power carried me through the first minute, but halfway through the second my arms felt like jelly. It was as if I had a two-ton lorry on my back. As I strained and strained to keep going, I actually saw that two-ton lorry crushing me. It was being driven by someone in a crazy red mask with yellow light beaming out of the eyes.

"You'll never do it," screamed the driver. "Never ... never ... never ... ha ha ha ha ha ha ha ha ha ha ha ha ha."

"I." *Push.* "Will." *Push.* "Do it!" I shouted out loud, much to the amusement, and bemusement, of everyone watching.

I kept going but I was in agony. My face was clenched in pain and the muscles in my shoulders felt like they would explode.

"Thirty seconds to go," Colin told me.

"Come on, Ade," said Salim. "You can do it."

I glanced again at my wheelchair over by the wall. As I bent my arms for one last press-up, I saw a small pulse of energy leave one of the wheels and travel along the floor.

A buzz went through me as I pushed up and straightened my arms just as Colin clicked down on his stopwatch and said, "That's it! Three hours – congratulations! You've done it!"

I couldn't speak. None of us could, but inside I was elated. We'd raised the first forty-one pounds and ninety-five pence towards my sports wheelchair.

Now all we had to do was raise the rest. Seven hundred and eight pounds and five pence to go.

9
Cheers, Jeers and Oh Dears

"ONE HUNDRED and thirty-six pounds and sixty-two pee, one hundred and thirty-six pounds and sixty-three pee, one hundred and thirty-six pounds and sixty-four pee."

"Have you finished now, Brian?" I asked wearily, having spent much of the past half an hour watching Brian count the money we had raised so far, and then count it again because he thought he'd missed a pile of two-penny pieces.

"Yes, that's definitely the total at the moment," he said. "Pretty good, isn't it?"

I had to agree it was.

Since the press-up-athon, we'd done a sponsored bike ride, a sponsored swing for four hours at the park, a sponsored hoopla (though Shed couldn't really get the hang of it and Dexter's hoop kept flying off) and we'd set up a stall outside school selling some of our old toys. We'd also sold ice pops every day, which had gone well because the sun had been shining for the last two weeks. The man in the corner shop had donated them to us after Brian and Shed told him he could be the person who helped a future huge worldwide Paralympian superstar get to the top. We were so close to the £250 deposit I needed to give Carlos – I'd decided not to worry about the rest of the money the chair cost right now. If Carlos could put the order in, I'd figure the rest out later.

Next up was a sponsored cheerathon.

It was Emily's idea. Melody's football trial was after school tomorrow and Emily had suggested that she teach us some routines and we could become official cheerleaders for Melody throughout the game. She reckoned the idea of watching a bunch of boys cheering and dancing on the sidelines would get people laughing and happy to put some loose change in a donation bucket.

Melody thought it might be embarrassing, but the rest of us loved the idea. She eventually agreed because, as Dexter pointed out, hearing the crowd chant your name is something real, professional footballers have to get used to.

After school we headed to the football pitch and found a spot by the halfway line. We'd worked out some chants at lunchtime and practised a few moves we were looking forward to trying out. Emily was doing lots to help us, and Brian had suggested that we ask her to become part of the gang. The others thought it was a good idea, but I wasn't sure. Even though my Cyborg Cat senses told me she was okay now, Emily had gone out of her way as the Night Spider to attack me. Could she really be one of the Parsons Road Gang? We always stuck together – could she have changed enough?

"Where's Melody?" I asked, looking at my watch.

"She should be here by now," Shed said. "The others are already warming up."

"Yeah, Spencer and his mates look like they're about to go to war," Dexter pointed out.

We glanced over to see them fist-pumping and shouting at each other with fierce determination on their faces.

"Maybe she needs a little bit of encouragement," I said. "Ready everyone?"

The others nodded and we burst into our first chant.

"Mel, Mel, Melody. Mel, Mel, Melody. Mel, Mel, Melody."

We kept going, but with kick-off fast approaching I could tell we were all wondering why she still hadn't appeared.

"There she is!" shouted Dexter as he spotted Melody coming out of the changing rooms.

We started chanting even louder, but it was obvious that something was wrong. She should have been sprinting towards the pitch, but she was trudging over as if there were weights attached to her feet.

As she came by us, we stopped chanting.

"What's the matter, Melody?"

"My lucky boots," she said dejectedly. "I can't find them anywhere."

"That's impossible," said Shed. "You definitely had them when you left home this morning – I remember you checking."

"I did," she said. "They were in my bag. But we had PE earlier and there must have been some sort of mix-up, because they're not in there now. I had to borrow this pair."

"They look all right," said Brian.

"Yeah," I said. "You'll be fine with them, Melody."

"But they're not my lucky boots," said Melody.

I was about to tell her that they were just normal boots and that she was such a good player she didn't need a special pair to score anyway, when Spencer and his mates came over.

"Seen my new boots?" sneered Spencer.

"They're Adidas, top of the range. All the professionals have them. What are you wearing, Melody?"

"Get lost, Spencer!" I shouted.

"Okay, okay, I just came over to wish her good luck," he said. "She's going to need it, ha ha ha." They all sprinted back to the centre of the pitch as the referee blew the whistle.

"Just ignore Spencer," I told her. "You're a great player, Melody. And with the Parsons Road Gang supporting you, you'll absolutely smash it!"

"Yeah," said Emily. "And we're going to be cheering for you the whole time! Mel, Mel, Melody. Mel, Mel, Melody..."

We all joined in, but as the game kicked off I didn't need superpowers to see that all was not well. Without her lucky boots, Melody's confidence was shot to pieces. The first three times the ball came to her she mis-controlled it, and then, just before half time, she had a great chance to score, but she hit the ball way over the bar.

Our cheerleading didn't seem to be helping at all. We kept it up throughout the first half and got quite a lot of donations, but I wasn't sure whether or not we should continue in the second half.

"We can stop chanting if you like, Melody," I said to her as she sat alone on the touchline eating a banana.

She was about to reply when we heard a horrible and familiar voice.

"What's the matter, looooosers?"

It was Spencer. Again. He'd come over to gloat.

"Are you sad because Wonder Girl has become Blunder Girl?" he continued meanly. "There's no way a gurrrl will ever make it into my team. Enjoy the second half, losers, ha ha ha!"

For a second, I thought Melody might throw what was left of her banana at Spencer, like she usually would, but then sadness returned to her face.

"You can't stop cheering, you need to keep raising money, Ade," she said.

"That's okay," I said. "We've got other things planned and if it's putting you off..."

"No," she said. "Keep going. At least then *something* good will have come out of today."

The second half started and we resumed our chanting with 'There's only one Melody Watson...'

Unfortunately, things didn't really improve on the pitch. Melody didn't play as badly as she had in the first half, but that was mainly because she kept out of the action. The few times the ball did come to her, she played very simple passes and then faded back into obscurity. She didn't do anything to make herself stand out.

Nonetheless, when she came off the pitch at the end we gave her a huge cheer.

"Well played, loser!" shouted Spencer, smirking, but we just cheered even louder to drown him out.

"Thanks, you lot," said Melody. "I just wish I hadn't lost my boots. I would have played much better with them on."

"If I find out who took them..." said Brian, making it very clear who he thought it was by shooting a look over at Spencer.

"You don't need the boots, Melody," I said.

"Thanks, Ade," she replied, "but I think I do. I played terribly today."

"That's because you *think* you need them," I said. "It's all in your mind."

"Careful," said Melody. "You're beginning to sound like Dexter with all his meditation and stuff."

"Oh-mmmmmmmmmmm," hummed Dexter, overhearing our conversation.

"Oh no," said Shed. "Now look what you've started."

"Oh-mmmmmmmmmm," continued Dexter.

We all covered our ears, expecting him to go on for ages, but for some reason he suddenly stopped.

"Oh dear," he said. "I think I might have got a bit too relaxed."

"What do you... Oh my goodness!" I shrieked. "That is the worst thing I've ever smelt. How many portions of beans did you have at lunch?"

"Only four," said Dexter.

"Quick – run!" I shouted. "Before we all pass out."

We charged away from Dexter, laughing. Even Melody was grinning and I felt pleased that we'd managed to cheer her up.

Unfortunately, that feeling changed very

quickly when I almost wheeled straight into my mother.

"Mum!" I shouted, startled. "What are you doing here?"

She didn't answer my question. She had a question of her own.

"Doyin, what is this about?" she said, handing me a piece of paper.

It was Emily's poster. There was a picture of all of us cheering Melody's name by the side of a football pitch, alongside the words, 'Sponsored Cheerathon: Raising Money for Ade's Sports Wheelchair'.

The others had taken one look at my Mum's expression and scarpered, leaving the two of us standing there by the football pitch. I didn't blame them. I'd have got away too if I could. I didn't know what to say.

"You know what we said about this, Doyin," said Mum.

"I know, Mum, but..."

"Hahh, Doyin." Her Nigerian accent was stronger than ever. "There can only be one reason why you want a sports wheelchair and your father made it very clear that we don't think you should be wasting your time playing basketball."

"But I'm good, Mum, really I am – the manager of the team saw me play and he thought so."

"I'm sure you are, Doyin," she said, and sighed. "It's great that you're raising money, but why don't you think about giving it to a proper cause, a charity or something? They would be very grateful and at least then it would be going to something important rather than this basketball nonsense."

"It isn't nonsense, Mum!"

"I know you don't think so, Doyin," said Mum kindly. "But will you at least consider what I've said? There are a lot of very deserving charities out there."

"Okay, Mum," I said. "Er, does Dad know about all this?"

"No, he does not. I haven't told him. Yet. But you know what he thinks. This basketball thing, it's not a good idea, not a good idea at all, Adedoyin."

PARSONS ROAD E13

BOROUGH OF NEWHAM

10
All in the Same Vote

"SHE didn't say you couldn't carry on fundraising, did she?" said Salim. "She just said you ought to think about donating the money?"

We were at the Parsons Road Gang emergency summit meeting that I'd called – I'd heard someone say 'emergency summit meeting' on television and thought it sounded good.

"That's true," I agreed.

"So I think we should carry on," Salim said.

"When we've got enough for your chair, we can think of something that will convince your mum and dad it's a good idea."

"Yeah," said Dexter. "You could show them some of your cool moves, like that 360-degree wheelie spin."

"Or that trick where you lift up on one wheel and skid round a corner," Brian said.

I wasn't convinced that was the sort of thing that would work with Mum and Dad, but I knew I didn't want to stop fundraising.

"Okay, let's put it to a vote," I said.

"Why?" said Melody. "We all agree."

"Because that's what people do when they want to decide things," I said. "And anyway, we don't know if everyone agrees. What do you think, Shed?"

"Eh?" Shed seemed startled, as if he'd just woken up from a dream.

"Do you think we should keep fundraising?"

"Oh, I can't right now, I've got to be home in fifteen minutes," he said.

We all laughed.

"Not right now, you silly sausage," said Brian. "Generally, should we carry on?"

"Oh, yeah. I guess so, yeah," he said.

"Right, well, now we're all in agreement," said Melody.

"I still think we should take a vote," I insisted.

"How about we take a vote about whether or not we should take a vote?" suggested Brian.

"Why?"

"Well," Brian said, "because we can't all agree that we want to take a vote on whether or not we think we should carry on fundraising, even though we do all agree we should carry on fundraising, so if we take a vote on whether or not to take a vote, then we can take a vote on whether or not to carry on fundraising. Or not. I think."

We all fell about laughing again at that.

"The main thing," said Salim, when we'd all stopped giggling, "is that the Parsons Road Gang are still on the case, and nothing is going to stop us raising the money for Ade's chair. Am I right?"

"Yes!" we all said, punching the air.

"Then the vote has been taken," he said, smiling.

We left in a good mood and, just over a week later, we'd raised even more money thanks to Melody's older brother and his cousin busking outside the local underground station, a book sale that we'd organised at school and a sponsored car wash.

Fundraising was going so well that Salim started to talk about what basketball chair I should think of getting.

"The Chevron 700 Baller!" he enthused. "It's by far the best on the market for the money you're gonna spend. Aluminium frame, 25-inch wheels and rollerblade front casters. You'll be unstoppable."

His excitement got me dreaming about the chair as well.

With just one minute to go in the Paralympic final, basketball's newest star, Ade Adepitan, takes to the court in his gleaming Chevron 700 Baller. With the game between Great Britain and the USA tied at 68–68, can he make the difference and write his name into the history books?

The crowd certainly think so! Just listen to that cheer as the referee restarts the match. Adepitan is immediately involved. He picks up the ball, weaves between two Americans and plays a beautiful pass to his teammate. Now he's off, charging forward, trying to evade his marker. This is incredible, I've never seen anyone manoeuvre a chair like this; it's like this player and his chair are one. His marker doesn't stand a chance, and, in fact ... Oh my goodness! The marker has become so disorientated by Adepitan's movement, his chair has toppled over. Now Adepitan is in the clear and, yes, that's a great pass back to him. This is it. If he can find the basket with this shot, Great Britain will become Paralympic champions. He's lining it up and ... there it goes. It's the perfect shot, through the hoop without touching the sides! Great Britain have won and it's all thanks to the brilliant Ade Adepitan!

At some point in the night that basketball dream must have turned into the zombie one and then into the waking nightmare of Brian pounding on my front door to tell me the news of his terrible discovery: that all the money had been stolen and I had a new nemesis, the Masked Marauder.

I was tempted to call another emergency summit meeting, but we had all gone to the park after getting together at the scene of the crime, so it was pretty much like we were having one anyway.

"It has to be someone on the basketball team," said Brian. "They've seen how good you are and they don't want you to join in case they lose their place."

"I know it seems the most likely explanation," said Salim. "But I can't believe any of those guys would do it. They all know how important getting a decent chair is."

Despite what Salim said, I couldn't help thinking about Tommy and what he'd said to me at the training session.

"Unless..." said Shed. We all looked at him. "Unless it's Emily. I mean, I know she's been really helpful, but you know what she was like before."

"Maybe that's her plan," said Dexter. "Be

really nice to us and then, bam! Destroy us from the inside."

"Rubbish!" shouted Melody. "She's really, really sorry about what she did. There's no way it's her."

It was good to hear Melody so certain about Emily, and my Cyborg Cat powers hadn't sensed any danger from her, but could the Night Spider have her own powers that prevented me from connecting to mine, so I didn't suspect her? I kept quiet.

"Well, whoever it is wants to stop us raising money, right?" said Salim.

"Right," we all agreed.

"So," he continued, "we should carry on raising even more money to show whoever it is that we can't be stopped."

"Yes," said Brian. "And to lure them out into the open."

"What do you mean?" Shed asked.

"Well," explained Brian, "we're doing a sponsored silence next. I think we should do it at the same time as the Rollers have their next training session."

"Yes," shouted Dexter. "We'll be so silent we'll be able to hear if any of the basketball players are talking about trying to stop us. It's brilliant!"

"Erm, I'm not sure that was Brian's plan," I said. "Or was it, Bri?"

"Not quite," said Brian. "School is about three miles from where the team train. Even if everyone between the school and the park were being silent and the players were speaking really loudly, I still don't think we'd hear them."

"So what is your plan?" asked Shed.

"It's very simple," said Brian. "A couple of us spy on the team while they're training. If anyone is missing and something happens during the sponsored silence..."

"Then the missing person must be the Masked Marauder!" shouted Dexter. "I knew that was the plan all along."

"Course you did," I laughed.

"Okay, but we need to make sure that everyone knows about the silence, which means we need Emily to make loads of posters," Melody said.

"But what if —?" Salim started to say what I was thinking.

"I guess this time we've really got to hope that she truly is on our side," I said. "Otherwise Emily is a lot more dangerous and evil then we ever thought, and we are in a lot of trouble."

CREDON
ROAD   E13

BOROUGH OF NEWHAM

11
The Silent Treatment

"**WOW,** Emily, how many posters have you made now?" I asked, looking at her latest offering, a picture of a large pair of lips with a finger over them and the word 'Shh' written above ... which actually may not be a word, now that I thought about it.

"I think that's the seventeenth," she said.

"Amazing," I told her.

She smiled and blushed a little, which made me feel really quite bad that we'd ever doubted her. I kept thinking about what Dexter had said, though, about her being really nice and then destroying us, so I stared hard at the poster. I was trying to get transported into it, like when I'd looked at the horrible graffiti Emily had made as the Night Spider. Nothing happened, apart from Emily looking at me a bit oddly, which made me blush.

I just didn't sense any danger at all. Emily was joining in with the sponsored silence too, which would make things very difficult if she actually was the Masked Marauder herself. No, I was certain that it wasn't Emily and more convinced than ever that she was definitely on our side.

The identity of my new nemesis was still a mystery, but whoever it was couldn't hide forever. Especially now that the Cyborg Cat, the Parsons Road Gang and the Night Spider were all on the case.

Salim, Melody, Emily and I had gathered in the music room for our sponsored silence as planned. A few minutes earlier we'd said goodbye to Brian and what had appeared to be a human shrub. The shrub was actually a heavily camouflaged Dexter. He'd painted his face green and stuck leaves and twigs all over his body in preparation for spying on the basketball team.

They were a little late leaving because Brian had borrowed his cousin's video camera and had spent ages setting it up. In fact, he would have taken longer if the rest of us hadn't all shouted, "Brian! Just turn it on!" A tiny red light was blinking at us from the camera. I didn't think it would be the greatest film of all time, but we'd have proof for our sponsors if we were successful keeping silent. They'd shuffled out with Brian in a bit of a huff and Dexter dropping bits of foliage as he went.

"I'm not sure Dexter's camouflage is all that helpful," said Melody. "It's fine if he stays in the bushes, but as soon as he steps away, you can see him a mile off."

"You can smell him a mile off most of the time as well," I said.

"Too right," said Salim. "Hey, where's Shed?"

"He had to speak to one of his teachers after lessons so I got the lift down on my own. He'll be here soon."

Sure enough, a few minutes later Shed appeared.

"Sorry I'm late," he said. "Have you started?"

"Yes we have," I said.

"Oh well ... hang on!" he shouted, realising what I'd done.

"Don't worry, Shed, you haven't ruined it!" I said, chuckling. "We're just about to start. Okay, everyone, time for the last words to come out of our mouths for two hours."

We all shouted lots of really bonkers stuff then. I screamed 'silly sausages and bum-bum bees' about six times, and Emily kept saying 'fluffy bunny bottoms'. We kept going for a couple of minutes, then, like a conductor of an orchestra, I gestured with my arms for everybody to gradually lower their voices until there was complete silence. We had begun.

It felt quite odd at first, the five of us just sitting there in complete silence under the watchful eye of the camera, but after fifteen minutes it became really peaceful. We weren't allowed to actually fall asleep, but before long I was having a fantastic daydream...

Many people have swum the English Channel, but no one has ever thrown a basketball across it. You have joined us today as this incredible feat is being attempted for the first time by basketball star Ade Adepitan. What's more, not only is Adepitan going to attempt to get the ball all the way across the sea from Britain to France, he is also going to try to score what would be the longest basket ever!

Adepitan is wheeling up to the edge of the famous white cliffs of Dover now. The basket is a mere twenty-one miles away in Calais. This is going to have to be some shot. He's taking a few deep breaths in preparation and he's just given the ball a kiss for good luck. Here goes. He's raising the ball up and with incredible power has released his shot.

The ball is sailing through the air at an amazing speed... Oops, nearly hit a seagull there... Now it's flying on, getting closer and closer to the French coastline... Yes, I can see the basket now, but will the ball reach it and, more importantly, will it go in?

It's getting nearer ... and nearer ... and nearer ... and...

It's in! What a shot! Ade Adepitan has scored the longest basket ever! What a player!

Unfortunately, my dream was interrupted when Spencer and two of his stupid mates walked in.

They didn't actually say anything, they just walked round and round, staring at us and going, 'Shhh shhh.' It felt really menacing, and very annoying.

I could tell we all wanted to shout at them, but none of us cracked. I think they were trying to decide who was most likely to, though, because eventually they decided to focus all their attention onto poor Shed.

They stood over him and Spencer kept staring right into his eyes. Shed looked really nervous and unsettled.

I wanted to scream at them to leave him alone, but I held back. I wasn't going to let anyone ruin our sponsored silence. We could always get them later.

My chair had other ideas, however. It suddenly started to glow with a raging intensity and before I'd stopped to think I had pushed down hard on the wheels and rolled right over Spencer's foot.

"Owwwwww!" he yelled, hopping about.

I was just about to sarcastically say sorry, when thankfully I remembered that I couldn't. Instead, I screwed up my eyes, put my fingers to my lips and shrugged my shoulders as if to say it was an accident.

"I hope you lot stay silent forever," he spat at me. "But even if you do you won't raise enough money because you're the biggest bunch of losers in the whole world. Come on, let's go."

Just as they got to the door, Spencer

decided to make one last attempt to catch us out.

"Watch this!" he shouted to his friends.

Pointing his backside in my direction he let rip with probably the loudest fart I have ever heard in my life.

Spencer's friends collapsed with laughter.

The rest of us had to cover our noises and mouths to stop ourselves from gagging on the rancid smell from Spencer's bottom.

"Now you're not just losers," shouted Spencer, "you're smelly lo–"

Spencer suddenly stopped in mid-sentence, which was unusual for him because he loved to gloat. He frantically started to grab at the back of his tight shorts.

"Oh no!" he cried.

Rrrr-rip!

That's when we all noticed that Spencer's vigorous squat and the force of his odorous expulsion had torn his shorts clean down the middle, exposing his Bob the Builder underpants.

Spencer's friends laughed even harder when they saw them.

"Shut up, the lot of you!" he screamed.

He covered the tear with his hand and started to scurry off, but then he stopped and pointed a finger at Shed. He was obviously trying one last time to get him to crack, but thankfully Shed kept his mouth shut and didn't say a word.

The next hour passed by peacefully enough, though there was a sudden burst of rain at one point that made a sound on the roof like loads of little balls being dropped from the sky. It startled Emily and she very nearly made a noise, but she clapped her hand over her mouth just in time.

With half an hour to go the mood changed. We were all looking at the clock, willing the time away. I suddenly felt as if I had so much to say, and I knew the others were feeling the same. The words inside my head were bursting to come out and it seemed harder and harder to stay silent.

The next twenty-five minutes were agonising, but with five minutes to go the end was in sight and I started thinking about the first thing I was going to say once the two hours were up.

I was deciding between shouting 'Silence, you are so over!' or, 'In your face, Silence!' when I heard a strange tap-tap-tapping coming from somewhere.

At first I thought it might be rain again, but this sound didn't seem to be coming from the roof.

"Aaaaaaarrgghhhhh!"

The terrible scream had come from Emily and, when I followed her pointing finger, I understood why.

Someone was at the window wearing a horrific ghostly zombie mask.

The Masked Marauder!

"Let's get him, quick!" I shouted, forgetting I was meant to be silent.

Melody was first to the door, but something was blocking the other side and she couldn't open it.

The rest of us joined her and together we pushed as hard as we could.

"Harder, harder," I bellowed. "He's getting away!"

Eventually we heard a scraping sound and the door opened. There had been four chairs propped up against it. The delay had allowed the Masked Marauder to get away.

"He's gone," I said dejectedly.

"Yes," said Salim. "But look."

He pointed to the ground by the window. Lying there was the mask my nemesis had been wearing. Sticking out from underneath it was a piece of paper.

"I'll get it," said Shed, picking it up. He handed it to me. "I'm pretty sure this is meant for you."

My chair started to hum and vibrate. I opened the note. This time letters had been cut out of a newspaper.

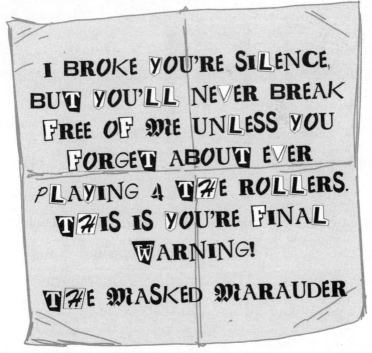

I BROKE YOU'RE SILENCE, BUT YOU'LL NEVER BREAK FREE OF ME UNLESS YOU FORGET ABOUT EVER PLAYING 4 THE ROLLERS. THIS IS YOU'RE FINAL WARNING!

THE MASKED MARAUDER

It was then that it really hit me. Not only had the Masked Marauder delivered another message telling me not to play for the basketball team, he'd also ruined our sponsored silence.

To make matters worse, when we checked the camera it was clear that our failure had been captured on film but, because the camera had been trained on us, there was no shot of the Masked Marauder at the window. With no money raised, it felt as if the sports chair was slipping out of my grasp. The Masked Marauder had won again.

Walking home, it was as if a gloomy black cloud was lurking overhead. We plodded along slowly and without talking. The shock of what had just happened had stunned us all back into silence. I was about to mutter goodbye to the others and slope off home when Brian and Dexter rocked up. Maybe they had the information we needed to unmask the Masked Marauder?

"He showed up," I told them. "The Masked Marauder came to the music room!"

"We thought as much," said Brian.

"Why?" asked Shed.

"We watched the team training," said Dexter. He was still heavily camouflaged, but a bit smudged and bare in places. "At first we thought they were all there, but that was only because Brian can't count."

"I can count," said Brian. "But not when I get interrupted all the time."

"I was only checking that you'd counted everyone," replied Dexter. "It's not my fault that you seemed to be missing someone out each time."

"I was not," said Brian. "You –"

"It doesn't matter," I said, worried that we'd be there all night if the two of them carried on bickering. "Just tell us the news."

"Okay, well, they weren't all there," said

Brian. "There was one person missing. I'm pretty sure it was someone called Howard. I remember him from when you played, Ade."

"You sure it wasn't Tommy?"

"No, Tommy was there, we saw him," said Dexter.

"Then Howard must be the Masked Marauder!" I shouted excitedly.

"Erm, I don't think so," said Salim.

"What?" I exclaimed. "It has to be him. Why don't you think so, Salim?"

"Howard's on holiday in Spain for a week. He's missing school and everything."

"But ... but if it's not Howard," I spluttered, "and it isn't anyone else on the basketball team, then who is the Masked Marauder?"

Once again, we were all silent.

12

Great British Cake Off

"ADE talking to the video camera to test it out, take seventeen. Action!"

"Brian," I said, "why can't you just say 'start'? It would be much easier."

"Because," said Brian, "that is not what real directors say."

"But you're not a real director," Melody pointed out. "And this isn't a real film."

We were getting things ready for our cake sale at the Parsons Road Street Party. It was held every couple of years to 'create a sense of local community', apparently. The Masked Marauder showing up at the sponsored silence, and ruining it, had only made me more determined to carry on raising money, and more determined to catch whoever it was. I'd decided I wasn't going to let anyone take away my dream. With my friends supporting me, I knew we were unstoppable.

We'd all made cakes to sell – with a lot of help from our parents, it had to be said. My mum had helped me make puff-puffs with a chocolate dip. Puff-puffs are like Nigerian doughnuts. The chocolate dip was Dad's special addition. When I asked for help, Mum gave me a look which said, 'I hope you've remembered that little chat we had about raising money,' but it seemed she hadn't told Dad anything yet. He was very pleased that I was getting involved in the cake sale. To be honest, I think he would have been happy for me to do almost anything else other than basketball.

Brian had brought the video camera along again. There was every chance that MM, as we'd started calling him, was planning to show up, and even though we were going to be on high alert, if he got away again hopefully Brian would be able to catch him on film so we could study the footage for clues. The only trouble was, Brian was acting as if he was a big Hollywood film director, and not a school kid who'd borrowed a camera.

"Melody," said Brian, "if MM shows up, I've got a big responsibility, so it has to be done properly. Look what happened at the sponsored silence when I wasn't there. You completely missed him."

"I've got a big responsibility as well," said Dexter. "If MM shows up, I've got to rugby-tackle him and then sit on top of him till you lot can take his mask off. Sooooo, I'm going to practise that now."

Dexter charged at Brian playfully and tackled him to the ground.

We stopped laughing when we noticed that the video camera was flying through the air. Dexter's tackle had been too enthusiastic.

It was as if the moment went into slow motion.

The others were frozen to the spot, but I felt like a bottle of pop that had been shaken, full of fizz and ready to explode. My mind was completely clear. I was Cyborg Cat and I could see exactly what I needed to do. In a flash, I zoomed over and just managed to grab the camera's strap before it hit the ground and smashed into a million pieces.

The others cheered, but I knew it had been a lucky escape.

"No more messing about," I said. "MM is

going to try something today – and, when he does, we need to be ready."

Over the next couple of hours, Parsons Road filled up with stalls and stages. It was going to be really busy, which would make it difficult for us to spot anything out of the ordinary, but we were prepared.

After the street party had been officially opened by the mayor, Emily and Shed took charge of the cake stall. Brian walked about filming, and me, Melody, Salim and Dexter stationed ourselves at places we'd decided gave us the best overview of everything. I stayed close enough to Salim to be able to pass a message on to him, and he was close enough to Dexter, who was close enough to Melody. Melody had also brought along her walkie-talkies and given one to me, so we had all bases covered when it came to communication.

As people started arriving at the cake

stall, the four of us kept scanning the scene for signs of possible MM activity. A lot of the younger children were getting their faces painted and seeing them wandering around with full face make-up was a little confusing, but as the crowds built during the first hour we were confident that my nemesis had kept away. It was early days, though.

The good news was the cakes were selling like hot cakes, although none of them were actually hot.

"How much have we made now?" I asked Emily. "And can I get a Vimto, please?"

I was taking my scheduled break from the surveillance team and I'd wandered over to the stall for a much-needed drink. Vimto was the first soft drink I'd had after we arrived from Nigeria and I just loved its blackcurranty taste.

Shed passed me a can. I handed him the walkie-talkie as I cracked it open. "Check in with Melody and get an update on how she's doing, would you?"

I gulped the cold drink down as I heard the walkie-talkie crackle as Shed made contact.

"I counted the money a few minutes ago," said Emily. "It was nearly forty pounds."

"That's amazing!" I said. "And there's still ages to go. So by the end we should have..."

I stopped. There seemed to be some sort of commotion. I glanced at the crowd and noticed that everyone was looking up and pointing into the sky.

The wheels on my chair began pulsing. I felt its energy pushing up through my hands and spine, calling to the cat within me. Something big was about to happen, I could sense it.

I shot a look up at the sky. There, floating above me, was a big bunch of colourful balloons. But that wasn't all. Tied just beneath them was a bag. My chair went ballistic. It felt like an emergency siren was going off in my head as shots of pure Cyborg Cat energy charged round my body, sending alarm signals from the tips of my toenails to the hair on my head. Whatever was inside the bag was Not Good.

I didn't have to wait long to find out. A moment later, an arrow fizzed through the sky and burst three of the balloons. The impact was just enough to send the whole bunch crashing to the ground. The bag landed with a thud and emptied its cargo. Masks!

There must have been hundreds of them, all different sorts. There were animal masks, cartoon characters, celebrities and film stars, scary masks and funny ones. Within seconds, all the kids – and plenty of grown-ups too – had grabbed one and put it on. There were now so many people wearing a mask it would be virtually impossible to spot the Masked Marauder amongst them.

It was a master stroke from an evil genius. Cyborg Cat had his work cut out.

"Brian," I shouted. "Are you getting this?"

From behind the camera, Brian gave me a big thumbs up.

I grabbed the walkie-talkie back from Shed and charged over to Salim.

"The Masked Marauder is here!"

"He must be," Salim agreed. "But what's he going to do?"

"I don't know," I replied. "Just keep watching as closely as you can. I'll tell Melody and Dex to do the same. This time he's not going to get away."

I tried to contact Melody, but for some reason she wasn't picking up. I scanned the crowd. By now most of the people at the street party thought wearing a mask was great fun and they were all giggling and messing about. It was chaotic.

I needed help. Cyborg Cat help.

I closed my eyes and tried to shut out everything around me. I slowed my breathing and focused my mind.

Cyborg Cat, I know you're in there, I can sense you. I need to catch the Masked Marauder and I need your help.

A moment later I saw a swirling ball of energy in my mind, like a Catherine wheel. Sparks were flying off it and zooming around my body, which felt electric.

We had connected.

Suddenly, everything got louder and clearer. I could make out people's heartbeats rhythmically beating like the drums from a marching band. I could pick out individual conversations and hear every word being spoken.

"How much for these lovely earrings? They'd be a perfect wedding present for my niece."

That was Mrs McLean, one of our neighbours. But the jewellery stall was at the other end of the street. How could I hear her so clearly?

"Woof! Woof! Grrrr..."

King, the German Shepherd that always chased us when we rode our bikes!

No way, I thought. King lived nearly two streets away. I couldn't be hearing him. But if he was roaming around here, things could get very scary. King hates kids.

I opened my eyes in alarm. There was no sign of a dog but it was as if I had super vision. I could cut through the crowds and hone in on tiny details. I could see the sweat on a woman's arm, a spot on a man's nose and, unfortunately, a small cloud appear from a boy's bottom when he farted.

It was a lot to take on board, and I was still trying to get used to my new powers when I spotted the Masked Marauder. Like a lot of other people in the crowd, he was wearing a panda mask, but I knew it was him. He was laughing to himself as he moved stealthily through the crowd. It was as if his body was surrounded by a dark, menacing aura that showed his bad intentions.

At first I couldn't see where he was heading, but then it became clear. He was making a beeline for our cake stall.

"Emily! Shed!" I shouted, but it was no good. They were really busy serving and didn't look up. They couldn't hear me above the crowd.

A moment later I saw the Masked Marauder duck round the back of the stall, grab the strongbox and try to walk off quickly. It was crowded, so he couldn't go fast.

Frantically, I tried the walkie-talkie again, but I couldn't get through. I was just about to hurl it to the ground in frustration when I noticed that the knob was tuned to the wrong channel. It must have got knocked. I clicked it back to the right position.

"Melody!" I screamed into the handset at the top of my voice. "Melody!"

"Ade, what's wrong?"

"Melody, the Masked Marauder has got the money and he's getting away! Get Dexter and head to the cake stall. I'll get Salim and Brian."

Moments later the five of us set off in pursuit. The chase was on.

The Masked Marauder was clever. He kept ducking in and out of the stalls and the crowd, making it difficult to keep track of him, even with my powers.

Dexter was haring around like a headless chicken, bumping into people left, right and centre. Unfortunately, one of those people was a man just about to throw a ball at the coconut shy. When Dexter barged into him, the ball the man was holding flew off in a very different direction to the one he'd intended it to. Thankfully, it didn't hit anyone. Somewhat less thankfully, it rolled onto a rug where a family were having a picnic. As I watched in horror, the grandmother of the family picked it up and, thinking it was an apple, took a big bite.

"Owwwwww!" she yelped as her false teeth came flying out of her mouth. Dexter had a lot of explaining to do and we were a man down.

I kept my eyes trained on the Masked Marauder. He was getting closer and closer to the end of the street. Once he was out of the crowds, his path would be clear and he'd get away.

"There!" I shouted, spotting a gap between a bouncy castle and a drinks stand.

We found ourselves with a clear run behind the stalls to the end of the street. If we were quick enough, we might just be able to get there at the same time as the Masked Marauder.

We zoomed down as fast as we could, Salim in front with me not far behind. Just as we passed the last stall on the street, Salim rolled over a rubber duck that must've fallen from one of the market stalls. It jammed into his front wheels, making a loud squeaking noise and forcing his back wheels up off the ground. It very nearly threw Salim out of his chair.

I was right behind him. Thinking quickly, I squeezed my push rims as hard as I could and managed to stop by doing a wheelie. I was literally millimetres from crashing into the back of Salim's chair.

The rest of the gang weren't so lucky. They clattered into the back of me, and I knocked into Salim, sending all of us flying into the air. We landed in a jumbled heap of tangled legs, spinning wheels and candyfloss. Brian had ducked down to avoid a rope and put his head right into a large stick of it that was being held by a young girl. The gooey pink mess was covering most of his head and quite a lot of the camera.

"Oh no," shouted Melody. "MM's getting away."

I looked up to see the Masked Marauder free of the crowds and running off.

"Not again," I groaned. "I can't believe it."

Feelings of disappointment and frustration started to overwhelm me, but then I felt my chair vibrate. It was trying to tell me something: *use your powers.*

I scanned the area with my super vision. I

didn't know what I was looking for but, as I focused in on a patch of long grass, I felt a jolt and I knew I'd found it.

"Melody, look!"

I pointed. In the middle of the grass you could just make out a football.

"What?"

"In the long grass. There's a football."

"So? What do you want me to do, Ade?"

"Take a shot," I said. "You're a brilliant footballer. You can stop him."

"I haven't got my lucky boots!"

"You don't need them, Melody," I said, looking at her. "You've just got to believe in yourself. You're the one with all the talent," I went on. "Not the boots. It's all inside you. I know you can do it."

Melody looked at the ball and then at the Masked Marauder, who was quite a long way away now, rounding a big tree close to the gates of the park. It was going to take something pretty special to stop him.

Suddenly, a look of real determination came over her face.

"Move back," she said to the rest of us.

We gave her the space she needed and watched as she took a deep breath and ran towards the ball. She glanced up one more time, focused in on her target and then let fly.

We watched as the ball curved round the tree and then bent back round to the other side of it. And then...

Thump!

It hit the Masked Marauder full on in the stomach, sending him sprawling to the ground.

It was the most incredible banana shot any of us had ever seen.

"Goooooaaaalllll!" cheered Brian. "Right, come on, let's go and unmask the Masked Marauder."

He looked around, but I wasn't there. I was already halfway to my nemesis as he lay defeated.

13
Masking for Trouble

I HAD imagined unmasking the Masked Marauder many times in my head. Usually, it had been a big, triumphant moment. I'd be in front of a crowd, shouting, "Behold, the true face of the Masked Marauder, captured by the incredible Parsons Road Gang!" Then everyone would gasp as they saw who it was and we would all be crowned heroes.

In fact, when I got to where he was lying I found myself feeling almost sorry for him.

He was lying on the ground, groaning. His mask was already half off and I could see what was probably sweat, but might have been tears, running down the side of his face.

"Go on then, Ade," said Melody, right behind me.

"Hold on – not yet!" Brian shouted. "First I need you to get into position. Go behind him, so you're not blocking the shot, and pull the mask off when I say 'ACTION!' Once the mask has been removed, Ade, I want you to give me a steely look straight down the lens. This, my friends, is going to be award-winning."

I raised my eyebrows a little. Brian was in full Hollywood film director mode.

Emily and Shed had temporarily closed the cake stall and joined us, and Dexter had sorted out his tricky situation by agreeing to wash the picnic family's car every weekend for the next month, so, with six pairs of eyes trained on me, I grabbed the panda mask.

In my imagination I'd whipped the mask off in one really cool move, but the reality was different. I didn't want to hurt whoever it was, so, slowly and carefully, I lifted his mask.

The dramatic gasping was just like I'd imagined it, though. As soon as the Masked Marauder's face was revealed, we all breathed in very quickly, and I made a slightly hoarse yelping sound.

It wasn't because of who it was, though. It was because of who it wasn't. Or rather, it was because of who it was, but who it was wasn't who any of us expected it to be.

None of us had any idea who this person actually was.

The man beneath the mask was a boy. He was a little older than the rest of us, but it wasn't anyone we recognised at all.

"Who are you?" asked Melody eventually.

The boy didn't answer.

"Why are you trying to stop Ade getting a sports wheelchair?" said Salim.

Still nothing.

"What have you done with all our money?" Dexter demanded.

Once again, the boy remained tight-lipped.

"This is ridiculous!" Brian groaned.

I raised my hand and gestured for calm.

"It's okay, Brian," I said. "We'll get him to talk."

"Oh, no, sorry," said Brian. "It's not him, it's this stupid camera. I've run out of battery. We might have to film those questions again when I've put the spare one in."

"We can't do it all again, Brian," I said, shaking my head in disbelief.

The Masked Marauder seemed determined not to say a word, but as I looked at him I felt a charge of energy from my chair. I closed my eyes and tapped into my Cyborg Cat self and a memory came back to me.

'I know you," I said. "You're Steph's brother. I've seen you in the playground at school. You're in the year above us."

He still didn't say anything, but that definitely hit home, I could tell.

"So now we know who you are," I continued, "we can go to the police and tell them about all the money you've stolen. We've even got your last theft on film."

"Indeed. We have a beautiful shot of you swiping the cash," said Brian, beaming. "It was magnificent – the dappled sunlight in the background created a real sense of drama."

"BRIAN!" I said sternly. This film director malarkey had totally gone to his head.

I don't know if it was the threat of the police or the glare I'd given Brian, but whatever it was it did the trick.

"I'm sorry. Please don't go to the police," the boy pleaded. "I only took the cash today, I don't know about any other thefts."

"Oh, so you can speak," said Dexter. "We thought for a moment that when you fell to the ground a worm had come along and eaten your tongue."

None of us had thought that. It was classic Dexter.

"So, go on then," I said. "Answer our questions."

"Look," the boy said, finally sitting up. "I don't know anything. Honestly. Someone slipped a message into one of my schoolbooks and asked me to meet them. They said they were a friend of Steph's."

"Rubbish," said Shed. "You're making it up."

"I'm not," he went on. "The message said that if I helped them I'd get enough money to pay for a really good pair of goalkeeping gloves. I really want to be the goalie in my year's football team. "

"Go on," I said. "So who did you meet?"

"That's just it," the boy said. "I don't know."

We all looked puzzled.

"When I met them they were wearing a mask," the boy continued. "A Darth Vader mask, so I couldn't tell who it was. They told me the plan: turn up here, burst the balloons, be the Masked Marauder and take your money. They said it was just a bit of fun for the street party, but that if I did it, they'd give me thirty pounds so I could get the gloves."

"You must know something about them," said Emily.

"Nothing," he said. "All I know is that whoever it was, they were quite tall. That's it. Please don't go to the police. Here's your money from the cake stall – take it. I don't know about any other thefts but I'll help you get the rest back too if you let me help. Please."

He took the moneybox out from inside his jacket and laid it on the ground.

It was a strange story, but I sensed he was telling the truth.

"You can go now," I said, picking up the box. "But you'll definitely be hearing from us again."

"Yeah, so don't think about leaving the country and going to live in Parazuela," shouted Dexter as the boy scurried away.

"I think you meant to say Paraguay," corrected Brian. "Or Venezuela."

"Right," I said, ignoring their bickering. "Time for another emergency summit meeting. Right now."

There were lots of suggestions about what we should do next. Brian wanted to hire the local cinema to show his film *The Great Capture*: A Brian Spielberg Production. He felt certain that whoever was behind the Darth Vader mask would come along to a premiere and give himself up. I wasn't so sure about that. Melody suggested that we throw a Star Wars party and check out all the people who turned up as Darth Vader. Salim suggested asking his uncle, who was a policeman, for advice, and Emily and Dexter chipped in but I noticed that one person wasn't saying very much at all.

"What do you think, Shed?"

"I don't know," he said. "It could ... I mean, the thing is, I..."

"Spit it out, Shed," said Dexter.

"Okay, well, look," he said. "All we know is that the person is tall, right?"

We all nodded.

"So, erm, that might mean that whoever it is could be ... a grown-up?"

That hadn't occurred to any of us.

"I suppose," I said. "But that doesn't help too much, Shed. Unless you have an idea which grown up it might be. Why would a grown-up want the money?"

Shed coughed.

"Er, well ... maybe ... the thing is..."

"Come on, Shed," said Salim. "Tell us. Who do you think it is?"

Shed looked at the ground before looking up at me.

"Ade, I think it could be your dad."

14
All Over It, Over

"SUSPECT leaving the house, over," I said into a walkie-talkie from my hiding place behind a parked car.

"I have eyes on the suspect." Dexter's voice came crackling back at me. "Well, one eye as I'm standing sideways on, over."

The suspect in question was Dad.

When Shed had suggested that the tall person in the Darth Vader mask might be Dad, I was shocked. I didn't want to even consider it.

If Dad didn't like something, he'd tell you straight. But when I told the rest of the gang that Brian pointed out that was exactly what he'd already done. Dad had said he didn't want me to play for the Rollers. End of. And I'd ignored him.

I argued back that Mum *had* said she hadn't told Dad about the fundraising for the chair, so if he didn't know anything about it, how could it be him?

The answer, according to most of the others, was simple. Mum had told him. As Salim said, parents are like that sometimes. They do what they think is best, but they tell you what you want to hear, when actually they've done something different.

I still wasn't convinced. If Mum had told him, why had Dad not just told me straight to stop fundraising? It felt like we were going round in circles.

Shed reckoned he had the answer to that one. He said after his dad lost his job, he'd wanted to tell the family straight away, but his mum had convinced him not to. She thought it was better not to worry everyone. Shed thought mums could pretty much convince anyone to do anything, especially dads. He thought my mum had told my dad that she would deal with it. Or maybe, that she had convinced him not to tell me straight but to let me down gently. So that's how they both came up with the Masked Marauder idea.

To me, there seemed to be more questions than answers, and we didn't have much to go on, apart from the Masked Marauder being tall. But when I'd tracked down Steph's brother again, whose name was Andy, he'd said that the person also had quite a deep voice. Like a grown-up.

Like my dad.

Try as I might, I couldn't come up with any other grown-up suspects. Everyone else was pretty supportive of my ambitions – the teachers at school had all sponsored us and loads of our neighbours. Dad was the only grown-up who made sense.

Being totally honest, I was shocked at the idea, but we didn't have any other theories. Once Shed had said it, I just had to know one way or the other, so I agreed that we should at least check it out.

The plan we'd come up with was this: Andy would contact the Masked Marauder to arrange to hand over the money he was supposed to have taken from the cake stall. Andy had told us that they'd previously met in the Chicken Basket, a fast-food restaurant on the High Street, on a quiet table near the back, away from prying eyes.

Andy would arrange the time and then we'd stake out my house to see if Dad left to go to the meet. If he did, Dexter and I would follow him and when Dad got to the restaurant... Well, I was going to have to confront him and then who knows what would happen.

On the other hand, if Dad didn't leave the house, we'd know it wasn't him. In that case, we'd decided that Melody, Shed, Salim and Emily would be waiting in the Chicken Basket, ready to pounce when the real Masked Marauder turned up.

Unfortunately, my worst fears had been confirmed. I lived about twenty minutes' walk from the restaurant and, sure enough, twenty minutes before Andy had arranged to meet the Masked Marauder Dad set off.

"Suspect is carrying a small rucksack," I said into the walkie-talkie. "Big enough to conceal a Darth Vader mask. Setting off in pursuit, over."

I just couldn't believe it. How could Dad be

the Masked Marauder? It was like a very bad dream.

I was following quite a long way behind, but Dad wasn't exactly rushing so it was easy to keep him in my line of vision.

After about two minutes, Dexter popped out from behind a bush and joined me.

"Suspect heading in the direction of the restaurant, over," he said.

"Dex, you don't need to say 'over' – you're right next to me."

"Oh. Okay," he said. "Over."

I shook my head.

"Come on. We don't want to lose him."

Trying not to draw attention to ourselves, we picked up our pace and saw Dad again as soon as we rounded the corner.

My guess was that he would duck into another building near to the restaurant to put the Darth Vader mask on, and then make his way to the meet with Andy.

When we got to the High Street Dad headed into the bank.

As we waited for him to come out, my wheelchair began glowing. This time, it wasn't red but green. Green for go. But did it mean go and confront him now, or did it mean go home? I was confused.

"He's taking a long time to put the mask on," said Dexter.

"Yes, he is," I said slowly. "You don't think he's gone out of a back door, do you?"

"Hang on," said Dexter.

He switched his walkie-talkie back on.

"Dexter to Melody, over."

There was a crackle from the walkie-talkie, then we heard Melody's voice.

"Receiving."

Dexter looked at me.

"She didn't say 'over,'" he said. "What should I do?"

"Just talk to her anyway, Dex."

"Okay. Melody, any sighting of MM yet? Over."

"Negative," she replied. "Andy still alone, no sign of MM. Repeat, no sign of MM."

Dexter didn't say anything again and looked at me.

"She didn't say 'over' again," he said.

I was about to tell him that it really didn't matter, but I'd had enough. What was Dad doing in the bank? I was determined to get to the bottom of it.

I pushed down hard on the wheels of my chair and charged towards the front door. I was just about to enter when...

Crash!

I banged right into someone coming out.

"Sorry, sorry," I started saying. "I was just looking for ... Dad!"

"Doyin?" Dad said. "What are you doing here? And why are you in such a hurry? Have you got a secret savings account that you are hiding from us?" He said it with a twinkle in his eye.

"Eh?"

I was confused. If Dad was the MM and on his way to meet Andy, why was he in such a good mood?

"If you have been hiding money, then I'll need at least ten years of rent from you."

He laughed loudly. Dad always enjoyed his own jokes.

"Oh no, erm, I wasn't," I spluttered, not knowing quite what to say.

"You certainly seemed to be in a hurry to go inside," said Dad.

Dexter came running up.

"We weren't following you, Mr Adepitan, honestly we weren't," he said, the words pouring out of him like a waterfall.

"Following me?" Dad looked confused. "I never thought you were."

"Oh good," said Dexter. "Because we definitely weren't. In fact, we definitely haven't been following you since you left your house twenty minutes ago, carrying a Darth Vader mask in your rucksack so you could take the money we've raised for Ade's sports wheelchair."

Dad looked at the two of us. It was a look I knew well. It wasn't a good one.

"Adedoyin," he said, "I don't know what it is you and your friends are up to, but it is time for you to have a talk with me and your mother. We're going home. Now!"

I didn't have a choice. As I left, Dexter made a face as if to say, 'What have I done?'

The answer to that, I thought gloomily, was 'got me into a whole lot of trouble'.

At home, I sat at the kitchen table facing a very stern and cross-looking Mum and Dad.

"Well?" said Dad.

I tried to think of lots of different reasons for being at the bank, and why Dexter would have said all that, but everything was a big muddle in my head, so in the end I just sighed and told them the truth.

"Adedoyin!" Mum shouted. "Why would you think your father would do such a thing?"

"It seemed to make sense," I whimpered.

"Only to you and your friends," said Mum. "Hahh! I've never heard such nonsense."

I looked down. I didn't feel good. I'd accused my dad of being a thief. Mum was scarily angry, but Dad was silent. Somehow that was worse.

"Adedoyin," said Mum sternly, "go to your room while your father and I have a talk."

"Yes, Mum," I said. "I... I... Sorry."

Sitting alone in my room I felt pretty stupid. I'd messed up. It didn't matter how strong my Cyborg Cat powers were or how good I was at basketball – if I made the wrong decisions, I'd never amount to anything.

I picked up a football magazine and flicked through it, but I couldn't really concentrate. I couldn't make out what Mum and Dad were saying, so all I could do was sit there and await my fate. No super Cyborg hearing for me now, I thought dejectedly.

"Doyin!" shouted Mum about half an hour later. "Come here, please."

I made my way downstairs with a heavy heart and a nervous stomach. I couldn't look at my parents and stared down at the ground as if my eyes were being pulled by extreme gravity.

"Doyin," said Mum. "Look at us."

My head felt like it weighed a ton, but I lifted it up slowly.

"We have been talking about your situation quite a lot," Mum continued. "Not just today, but over the past few weeks and ... well, why don't you tell him, Ajibola?"

Dad looked at me. I expected to see a fierce anger in his eyes, but it wasn't there. I was relieved, but also confused.

"Adedoyin," he said, "I'm still not exactly sure what you thought I was doing earlier, but the fact that you seemed to think I might be going to steal money from you, that I do not like. It upsets me greatly."

"I know, Dad, but…"

He held his finger up to silence me. There was more he wanted to say.

"I hope you know that I would never, never do anything like that."

I nodded.

"Good," Dad said. "Now, you also know that I have found it difficult seeing you in a wheelchair, Doyin."

I nodded again.

"But, over the past few weeks, I have noticed how well you have been doing in it, how determined you are, and that makes me very proud."

I smiled, taken by surprise.

"I really do believe you can do anything, whether you're in a wheelchair or not, and I do mean anything."

This was going well now.

"Does that mean you don't mind me being in the basketball team?" I asked, still a little unsure.

"No, I don't mind," said Dad. "I can see how much it means to you. So you can play. On one condition."

"Yes, Dad?"

"You must concentrate on your studies, and at the end of each term you must get As in all of your classes. I will speak to your teachers. If they tell me that you have been messing around or not working hard enough, there will be no more basketball."

"Yes, Dad," I said forlornly. Getting top marks at school was going to be tough.

"Oh, and one more thing," he said. His voice was stern again. "You had better be the best player on the whole team. I want you to get an A in basketball as well. If Coach Carlos tells me you're not working hard there will be trouble."

I was in shock. "H-how do you know Coach Carlos?"

"Doyin –" this time it was Mum's turn – "don't worry. Just do as your father says."

She smiled and gave me a wink.

"Yes, ma'am! Yes, sir!" I said, saluting with a huge grin on my face.

I hadn't expected this. I was so happy I almost cried. It was such a relief to know Mum and Dad believed in me.

I was in such a good mood I was just about to ask Dad if he wanted to throw a ball around with me. That was until I suddenly remembered.

Dad wasn't the Masked Marauder.

That meant whoever it really was must have turned up at the restaurant to meet Andy. With any luck that also meant it was time for another unmasking.

15

In a Restaurant Not So Far, Far Away

"WHERE is he? Where's Darth Vader? It's time to defeat him and his evil empire."

After what had happened with Mum and Dad, I was absolutely buzzing when I got to the Chicken Basket. It didn't last long.

"He's not here," said Brian. "He didn't show up."

"We've been sitting here the whole time," said Shed.

"Yeah," said Melody. "And Andy hasn't moved either."

Andy gave me an awkward wave from a nearby table.

"I contacted him, honestly," he said. "But it's just an answering machine. I left a message. It's always worked before."

"Dex told us what happened with your dad," said Salim. "So we thought you, erm, might not be in such a good mood."

"Yeah, I thought I wouldn't be either," I said. "Dad wasn't happy about me thinking he'd taken the money, but, get this – he's completely changed his mind about me playing basketball!"

"That's amazing, Ade," said Melody.

"I know, it's brilliant!"

"But, Ade, the Masked Marauder didn't turn up here and your dad didn't turn up here," said Shed. "So doesn't that mean it could still be your dad?"

"No way," I snapped. "Dad and Mum are both completely behind me getting a sports wheelchair. They want me to do well so why would they try to stop me?"

"So who's left as a suspect?" Emily asked. "What's our next move?"

I really didn't know. It felt as if we were back to square one. Who was Andy's mysterious, evil boss? None of us had any idea. There was only one thing for it.

"Emergency summit meeting," I said.

"Not another one," groaned Salim.

"Yes," I said. "We're the Parsons Road Gang and when we put our heads together we can solve any problem!"

Everyone punched the air and cheered, even Andy – although he clearly didn't know what we were on about.

Despite the fact that my nemesis was still a mystery, it felt good to be with my friends. I knew we would figure this out.

"Excuse me."

One of the restaurant's employees was standing by our table.

"You've all been here for ages and only had a bag of chips and one drink between you. If you're not going to buy anything else, my manager says you have to leave."

chicken basket

As we all got up to go, Shed said, "Hey, why don't we have the meeting at my house?"

I was pleased. Shed hadn't invited us to his house since his dad had lost his job, so maybe this was a sign that things were getting better for him and his family.

We said goodbye to Andy – with Dex reminding him once again not to leave the country or escape to Hungamania – and set off back to Parsons Road, mucking about on the way as usual. Halfway there, though, Melody pulled me back from the others. Something was on her mind.

"Why didn't the Masked Marauder turn up?" she said.

"I don't know," I replied. "Perhaps he knew that you lot were going to be there."

"That's what I've been thinking," she said. "But how?"

"Andy could have told him, I suppose," I said, but I knew I didn't really believe that.

"Maybe," she replied. "But listen, Ade, if not, the only other way he could have found out is if one of the gang told him."

"What?!" I shouted so loudly the others turned round.

I laughed it off, but as soon as they'd started mucking around again I turned back to Melody.

"No way," I said. "No one in the Parsons Road Gang would do that."

"I agree," she said. "But I don't mean on purpose, of course. I mean by accident. Maybe one of his friends overheard us talking?"

"It's possible," I said. "Let's see what the others say."

We headed up to Shed's bedroom for the emergency summit – the others helped me and Salim get upstairs. I kicked it off by recapping what we knew – not a lot – and then I asked if any of them could have been overheard talking about our plan to ambush the Masked Marauder at the Chicken Basket.

None of them could recall doing that. Brian said he'd spoken to Dexter about it on the phone, but he'd taken the phone up to his bedroom and spoken really, really quietly under his bed.

Dexter suggested that the government might have been listening in to the call.

"I think they've trained Dr Snuggles," he said.

We all stared at him, open-mouthed.

"Dex! What are you talking about?"

"Dr Snuggles, my sister's cat!" Dexter said, looking at us like we were the idiots. "He meowed very loudly when Brian called me. And he was staring at me from the stairs. It could have been Dr Snuggles who told MM about the plan."

"Dr Snuggles is a talking spy cat that works for the government? And may have informed MM about our plan?" Brian replied, his hands on his head in total disbelief.

"Yeah, I know, it's an absolute cat-astrophe!" Dexter said casually.

They all cracked up.

"Come on, you lot, stop messing around," I said impatiently. We had to get serious if we were going to find out who was behind the Darth Vader mask.

Knock knock.

It was Shed's mum.

"It must be hungry work doing whatever it is you're doing," she said. "Dad's had some good news and we're celebrating. He's going to the fried chicken shop, so would you all like something?"

Everyone nodded eagerly. They'd only had money for chips earlier, and watching other people eating chicken had made them desperate for some.

"Shehzad, could you make a list of what everyone wants?" his mum said. "Quickly, Dad wants to set off soon."

Shed seemed a little embarrassed that his mum had called him Shehzad. My mum and dad always call me Doyin or Adedoyin instead of Ade – it must be a parent thing. Nobody batted an eyelid, though, and Shed got on with the job in hand, which actually wasn't all that easy.

"Can I have a three-piece bucket of chicken, please?" said Emily.

"Sounds good," said Salim. "I'll have one as well."

"Actually, you can't," said Dexter.

"Yes, they can," said Shed.

"Yes," I said. "In fact, I'll have a bucket of chicken as well please, Shed."

Dexter shook his head.

"No, Ade, you can't. None of you can."

"Dexter's gone bonkers," laughed Melody. "He's turned into the Fried Chicken King – only he can decree who can and can't eat chicken."

"I like the sound of that," chuckled Dexter. "I think my name would be King Cluck the Third. But that's not it."

"Well, what is it, Dex?" shouted Brian. "I'm starving!"

"And my dad's waiting," added Shed.

"None of you can have a bucket of chicken," Dexter said, "because the shop doesn't do a bucket of chicken. The clue is in the name of the shop. Chicken Basket. It's a basket of chicken."

We all threw whatever we could find at Dexter, which meant three pens, a pack of cards, two pillows and a lot of Lego.

"Right," said Shed finally. "Who wants a basket of chicken?"

Four of us put our hands up. Shed wanted chicken with chips, Melody wanted chicken wings, and Dexter, believe it or not, didn't even want a basket. He wanted a chicken burger and chips.

As Shed started writing down the order, I started to feel very odd. My head began to throb and I felt really scared something wasn't right. I couldn't work out what was going on.

Shed left to find his dad and when I looked up Emily was staring at me. No one else had noticed my distress.

"Are you okay?" she mouthed, trying not to let the others see.

Could Emily sense it too? Or was she making me feel weird – was she trying to use her Night Spider powers to destroy me again? Even worse, had Emily managed to totally fool us: was she the real Masked Marauder?

The throbbing in my head got worse. Shed's room suddenly started to go all hazy and a swirling wind whooshed around me. I thought I might faint or throw up, but then a gap appeared in the haze and my senses were drawn to a poster on Shed's wall.

Above me, Luke Skywalker seemed to be pulling me nearer and nearer to him. Or perhaps he was coming towards me. I couldn't tell.

Using all my mental strength, I tore myself away from the poster. The haze began to fade, but a strange and uncomfortable thought had crept into my head.

No, that's ridiculous. Loads of people like Star Wars. I have posters of the film on my bedroom walls too.

The thought wouldn't go away, though. The throbbing in my temples was getting stronger. My body was tingling and the word 'close' kept repeating itself over and over in my head. *Close. Close. Close.* Was I close to what I was looking for? Maybe then this stupid headache would stop.

Usually, my Cyborg Cat powers gave me strength, made me feel undefeatable. This time it felt different. I was sure my chair was buzzing and glowing downstairs, but I wasn't in it, and I couldn't even see it. I felt out of control. Instead of excitement, I felt nervousness and dread. A moment later I found myself moving towards Shed's bed. I couldn't stop even if I'd wanted to.

I put my hand underneath the mattress and felt around. I brushed against something and pulled it out.

A mask! A Darth Vader mask!

That didn't prove anything, I told myself desperately. *Star Wars* was a massive blockbuster; the stuff was everywhere. I bet Shed didn't even remember he had this mask...

Suddenly, the laughter I had heard when I'd found the first clown mask came back again.

Hahahahahahahahahahahahahahahahahaha!

The laughter was loud but there was something else too. I concentrated hard, focusing in. I could hear a different word being repeated now.

Order order order order order order order order order.

Suddenly, I knew what it meant. Shuffling on my backside, I pushed past my friends and out of the door, clutching the side of my head in agony.

"Ade!" shouted Salim. "Where are you going?"

I didn't have time to answer. I slid down the banister and got into my chair. It felt good to be reunited with my two-wheeled companion and I raced to the front door. Shed's dad was in the car, but I managed to bang frantically on the window. He turned and saw me.

"Ade," he said. "What's the matter?"

"I'm sorry, Mr Akram," I spluttered breathlessly. "Can I have a look at the order, please?"

"Of course," he said, handing it over. "Did you want me to get some more chicken? You need to keep your strength up if you want to get into that basketball team. Shehzad tells me those boys are very strong. He worries about you, Ade, you know."

I didn't answer. By now my headache was so bad I could barely hear what Mr Akram was saying. I looked down at the order.

chicken and chips.
chicken wings.
chicken burger and chips

Then I saw it.

Barsket of chicken x 4

Barsket. That was the spelling mistake that had been on the first note I'd got, the one that had come with the clown mask.

An eerie, cold feeling came over me.

I had discovered the identity of Darth Vader.

chicken basket

16

Chicken, Chips and Spilled Beans

SHED.

It didn't make sense. I felt my Cyborg Cat senses powering down and my headache easing off. I'd finally got the right answer but...

Shed?

I was making my way very slowly back up the stairs, feeling dazed and confused when the bathroom door opened.

"Oh, hi, Ade."

Shed had been in the toilet when I'd charged out to the car, so he hadn't seen me desperately rushing to get to his dad before he drove off.

I looked at him. A million thoughts whizzed around my head, but in the end I just said, "It's you, Shed. You're Darth Vader. You're the Masked Marauder."

He reacted as if I'd punched him. He reeled backwards and put his head in his hands.

"I'm sorry, I'm sorry, I'm sorry," he kept saying over and over.

I was pleased he wasn't denying it, but I didn't like seeing Shed like that. He was one of my best friends. I was confused and hurt. Most of all, I just felt really sad.

"It's okay, mate," I said. "Just tell me why."

"It's not okay," said Shed. "It's not okay. I should never have done it and then it got out of hand and now we're in a real mess."

"What got out of hand?" I said. "Shed, I don't understand."

"No," said Shed, suddenly standing up straight. "I'll tell you everything, Ade, but not just you. I'll tell everyone. And then ... well, then you can kick me out of the Parsons Road Gang."

"We'd never do that," I said, and I meant it. Whatever it was that Shed had done, he'd always be part of our gang. I knew the others would back me up.

We headed back to his room in silence.

"Hey, where's my chicken?" shouted Dexter.

"It ... it's not here yet," said Shed, looking down at the floor.

The others could tell straight away that something was up.

"Erm, Shed has got something he wants to tell us," I said. "Go on, Shed."

He took a deep breath.

"I ... I'm Darth Vader."

"What?!" yelled everyone, pretty much in unison.

"Don't be a silly sausage, Shed," said Brian. "You can't be."

"I am," said Shed quietly. "And I was the original Masked Marauder. The money that was stolen from Brian's shed and the clown mask and the message – it's all my fault."

There was a stunned silence. No one could quite believe it. Emily was the first to speak.

"Why, Shed?" she asked quietly.

"I-I did it because ... because ... " Shed looked down. "Because I was jealous."

"Jealous?" said Dexter. "What were you jealous of?"

Shed kept looking at the floor.

"I was jealous of Ade getting more friendly with Salim," he mumbled. "It felt like he didn't need me any more. I thought if Ade joined the basketball team that would be it, and we wouldn't be friends."

I didn't know what to say. I looked over at Salim, who seemed horrified. The others were open-mouthed.

"So I came up with the idea of the Masked Marauder," went on Shed. "And I was going to do it myself, I wrote the note and everything, but I couldn't ... I couldn't take the money."

Shed took a deep breath and continued.

"That's when I contacted Andy. His dad works ... well, worked with mine. They both got laid off at the same time, so I knew his family wouldn't have much money. Steph had told me how upset her brother was because now he wouldn't get the goalie gloves he wanted and that gave me the idea."

Shed paused. We were all gobsmacked and hanging off his every word.

"I secretly put a note in one of his books asking him to meet me if he wanted to make some money. I didn't even know if he would turn up, but he did. I couldn't reveal my true self to him, though, so I wore the Darth Vader mask and spoke in a deep voice."

"Wow," said Brian. "This is like a film."

"Shhh," hissed Dexter. "Go on, Shed."

"He thought it was a joke at first, but I said he could have thirty pounds for the gloves so he agreed. He didn't ask me why or anything, and I was going to use money from my savings to pay him. I always meant to give the money we'd raised back."

We couldn't believe what we were hearing.

"I bought another strongbox. They all have the same key you see..."

"Told you," said Brian.

"Shhhh," said the rest of us.

"Yeah, anyway," continued Shed, "I gave it to him, so he could easily take the money. Then I met him again in the restaurant so he could hand it over. It was the same table right at the back – I didn't think anyone would see us."

Shed was getting a bit agitated now.

"So who saw you?" I asked.

"One of Spencer's mates – Gavin. He was getting takeaway and he clocked us. Well, he clocked Andy and someone in a Darth Vader mask. He didn't know it was me then."

"I knew Spencer had to be involved

somehow," I said angrily. "What happened then, Shed?"

"Yeah, well," he said, "the next day at school, Gavin and Spencer and a couple of others had a word with Andy, if you know what I mean."

We knew what he meant.

"So Andy left me a message. I'd given him my cousin's phone number and told him if he needed to get in touch to leave a message on the answering machine. He asked me to meet him the next day back at the restaurant because there'd been a problem."

"Spencer had taken all the money!" shouted Melody.

"It's worse than that," said Shed. "Andy wasn't there when I arrived, so I waited, and then Spencer and his mates turned up. I tried to get away, but there were four of them. They made me take the mask off. They

couldn't believe it was me either – they just laughed and laughed."

Suddenly, I heard it.

Hahahahahahahahahahahahahahahahahahaha.

My whole body reacted to the laughter this time. Rather than fear, I could feel myself pulsating with anger. I could handle it when Spencer and his mates went after me, but when they picked on my friends it was like an attack on my family.

"They made me tell them what I'd done," Shed continued. "They laughed again – they thought it was great and even suggested I should join their gang. I thought they'd had their fun, but Spencer suddenly stopped laughing and looked at me."

I could just picture Spencer's froggy little face staring right at Shed. It made me even angrier thinking about it.

"He said that if I didn't keep stealing the money he'd tell you everything, Ade. I said

I didn't care. I'd already decided to tell you anyway, but he said he'd go to the police, and then my family would get involved..." Shed gulped. "Well, with everything that's been going on, I couldn't let that happen. Mum and Dad had enough to worry about. So ... so I agreed."

Shed was staring hard at the ground now. We were all looking at him, but I knew none of us were angry. We all felt sorry for him.

"Blockmail!" shouted Dexter suddenly.

"What?" said Salim.

"Shed is being blockmailed by Spencer. You know, it's where they stop you getting any letters unless you do what they say."

That properly broke the tension and we all burst out laughing.

"It's blackmail, you dozy dummy," said Melody, tears rolling down her face.

"Oh yeah," said Dexter. "So what's blockmail?"

We all laughed again, but I noticed that Shed didn't join in. He was taking lots of deep breaths, desperately trying to hold back his tears.

"It's probably best if you all leave now," he said quietly, opening the bedroom door.

"What?" we all shouted in disbelief.

"After everything I've done, I don't deserve to be part of the gang. I know you must all want me out. So I think you'd better go, okay?"

"No way," I replied. "Not okay, Shed. I meant what I said before – we'd never kick you out of the Parsons Road Gang."

"Yeah," Melody said, stepping in front of him. "What happened was a mistake, Shed, we can sort this."

"But after what I've –"

I didn't let him finish.

"Shed, just because I'm getting more confident in the chair doesn't mean I don't want you to be my friend. When I first moved to London I felt really scared and lonely. I didn't think I'd ever have any mates here, because I'm different."

I sighed and looked down at the metal caliper on my left leg.

"But, Shed, you didn't care about that." I looked at the others. "None of you did. I'm really lucky to have you all as my friends. If you leave now, Shed, the Parsons Road Gang will never be the same."

As I finished talking I heard sniffing. It was Dexter. He had tears in his eyes. Salim put one of his big hands on Dex's shoulders.

"You okay?" he asked.

"Sh-Shed," Dexter said. "I really want –"

"Don't worry, Dex," Shed replied, obviously worried. "I'm gonna stay – if you really want me to."

"I know you are, Shed," Dexter said. "It's not that. I really want my basket of chicken.

When is your dad going to get back? I'm wasting away!"

With that, Dexter dramatically threw himself onto the floor and burst into tears.

"Are you lot always so emo?" Emily said, looking perplexed. I guess she was still getting used to being around the gang.

"I can't believe you weren't upset because you thought I was leaving the gang!" shouted Shed. "There's only one punishment for that. Bundle!"

Before anyone could say any more, Shed jumped on Dexter, followed by the rest of us, all laughing and shouting in a massive heap on the floor. I was relieved. The Parsons Road Gang were staying together.

"So, what are we going to do then?" asked Melody, picking herself up and dusting herself down.

"Well," I said. "I thought..."

"No, please, no," said Salim. "Not another

emergency summit meeting."

"Well, technically," Brian remarked, "we're still having one now, so it wouldn't actually be another one."

"Knock knock." It was Shed's dad. "Chicken's here," he said cheerily.

"Woo-hoo! Make way! Talented and hungry boy coming through," Dexter screamed as he steamed over to Mr Akram, making sure he was first in line for his basket of chicken.

After a long day, and all the drama, hot fried chicken was just what we needed.

"Right," I said, after I'd polished off my chicken. "We can't let Spencer and his horrible mates get away with this. We need a plan. Any ideas?"

No one said anything at first, but then...

"I've got an idea."

It was Shed.

17
Wheelchairs, Attack!

I WAS in the park, hiding in the bushes.

About fifty metres away, I could see Spencer and Gavin, standing opposite Shed.

Shed had asked to meet just Spencer, so Gavin being there complicated things a little, but it didn't matter. We were going ahead as planned.

"So what is it?" sneered Spencer. "What are you going to do this time and why do you need to talk to me about it?"

"I'll tell you what I'm going to do this time," said Shed bravely. "Nothing."

"What do you mean, nothing?" said Gavin.

"I mean nothing," said Shed. "I've had enough of this. I've had enough of your blackmail. I'm not doing anything any more."

"I see," said Spencer. "Well, then, Gav, me old mate, you know what that means, don't you?"

Gavin gave Spencer a bemused look.

"Er ... it means we're going to, er ... throw him into the paddling pool?" he said.

"Yeah, yeah," said Spencer. "We'll do something like that, Gav, but not before we tell his peg-leg best mate Ade everything. Or maybe I should call him creepy cripple crawly? I'm sure Ade will be very interested to find out you've been stealing the money for his stupid sports wheelchair."

Spencer and Gavin began to cackle like a pair of wild hyenas. I could see Shed's fingers on his left hand curling into a fist.

"Don't do it, Shed – they're not worth it. Stick to the plan," I whispered, willing him not to react.

For a split second I thought Shed was definitely going to do something stupid, but then, to my relief, the expression on his face changed.

"You wouldn't!" said Shed, looking shocked. He was actually a pretty good actor when he needed to be, I thought. He'd had us all fooled for ages, I guess. Spencer ought to be easy after that.

"Course I would," sneered Spencer. "Unless you change your mind about not carrying on."

Shed look at Spencer intensely for a few seconds. Then he relaxed completely.

"Nah, it's fine, you can tell him," he said, as if he didn't have a care in the world.

"What?" shouted Spencer.

"Yeah, go on, then, tell him," repeated Shed. "Tell Ade."

That was the cue we'd been waiting for.

Before Spencer or Gavin could say anything else, a wheelchair came out of the bushes opposite me. The person sitting in it was wearing a mask.

"Go on then, tell me."

Then another wheelchair popped out of the bushes. The person in this one was also wearing a mask.

"Yeah, go on then, tell me."

Then another wheelchair appeared, and another, and another, until eventually Spencer and Gavin were surrounded by masked people in wheelchairs all shouting, 'Tell me, tell me.'

The look on their faces was priceless. They looked completely confused and absolutely terrified.

Finally it was my turn. I burst out from the

bushes, into the circle of wheelchairs, and went right up to Spencer. I wasn't wearing a mask.

"Go on then, tell me," I said.

Everyone laughed, except Spencer and Gavin, of course. They turned to run off but were blocked by an army of wheelchairs.

"And we want ALL the money back!" I shouted. "Or we'll be the ones going to the police!"

A couple of the guys in the wheelchair circle moved out of the way and we watched Spencer and Gavin leg it out of the park. There was a huge cheer and everyone took off their masks.

Shed's idea had worked perfectly. Getting all the players from the basketball team to help was a master stroke.

"Boom! Parsons Road Gang and Newham Rollers one, Spencer and his stupid mates a big fat nil!" shouted Dexter, emerging from the bushes with Brian, Salim, Melody and Emily.

"Yup," I said, a huge grin on my face. "But we couldn't have done it without Shed. What a performance!"

"Oh, well, you know, I just ... It was..." spluttered Shed.

"Hey, you're meant to give the speech after you've got the award," I said.

"What award?"

Brian stepped forward and cleared his throat.

"Ahem," he said. "Ladies and gentlemen. Welcome to the Oscars. The next award is for Best Performance by a Member of the Parsons Road Gang. And the winner is..."

He opened an envelope that he'd been holding in his hand.

"Shehzad Akram!" he shouted.

Emily stepped forward holding a statuette made out of tin foil and old toilet rolls. It was really good. It looked just like one of the real Oscars as it shimmered in the light. I could see Emily had worked some of her magic on it. She handed it to Shed.

He looked completely bemused, but he took it and held it up. It had some words on it that we'd written especially.

Winner: Shed
Member of the Parsons Road Gang
FOREVER!

"Make your speech," I whispered to him.

"I ... I don't know what to say," he said. "I ... thank you, you lot really are the best mates anyone could ever, ever have."

Everyone cheered again. And clapped and whistled.

"But, erm, I also want to specially thank Salim, cos, well, without the basketball team helping today we wouldn't have been able to pull this off and, I know it was my idea, but it was him who got them all to come along, so thanks, Salim."

Salim and Shed high-fived each other, then someone produced a basketball and suggested a match. Perfect.

We were going to choose teams in the normal way, with two captains picking players one after the other, when I had a better idea.

"How about the Parson's Road Gang versus the Newham Rollers?"

It took a moment for it to sink in, but then Dexter shouted, "Yeah, you'll never beat us, we'll destroy you," and the game was on.

I wasn't convinced we'd win, but it was great playing with the Parsons Road Gang. My friends might not be the best basketball players, but we had a bond, and an understanding, which meant we weren't half bad. I was on great form and Salim was part of our gang, not one of the Rollers today, so when we stopped for a break, we were only four points behind.

"Okay," said Salim. "When we start again I want Shed and Ade to pair up and move forward together. When I shout 'now', split up and go in different directions to the basket. Hopefully, it'll confuse them and they'll only stay with one of you, leaving the other one in the clear."

When the game started again it was like me and Shed were glued together. Wherever

I went, he went. As Salim had suspected, the Rollers were confused by this, so when we split up on Salim's command they marked me and left Shed in the clear.

Salim found him with a great pass. The shot was on.

Shed eyed up the basket. He lifted the ball above his head and then he let fly.

"Yes!" The ball sailed straight into the basket.

"Way to go, Shed," said Melody.

"Great shot," said Brian.

"Yeah, you did well," said Salim.

"In fact, you're all doing pretty well. If you're lucky, one day I might teach you guys how to play basketball in wheelchairs."

"Thanks, Prof," said Dexter. "And if you're lucky, I might give you a masterclass in football."

"Yeah," I said. "A masterclass in how not to play football."

We played until it became too dark to see the ball – the Rollers won, but only by seven points. As we were leaving, Tommy came up to me and said he was sorry about what he'd said before and that it was good to have someone like me in the squad. He did also say that he wasn't going to Dublin again anytime soon, but he was smiling, so I think he's looking forward to some healthy competition. We shook hands with the Rollers and headed for home.

Incredibly, everyone still had enough energy to race back to Parsons Road (and I won that one!).

The next morning I was up early when the doorbell went.

"I'll get it," I yelled and headed to the front door.

When I opened it, there was no one there.

"Hello? Hello?"

I was about to go back inside when I looked down. There was a strongbox on the ground. Smiling to myself, I picked it up and went back to the breakfast table.

"Who was it, Doyin? And what's that?" Mum asked.

I opened the box.

"Goodness me!" said Mum. "Doyin, that

is a lot of money. Where has it come from? How much is there?"

I knew exactly how much it was, but I counted it out, just to be sure.

"One hundred and eighty-six pounds and forty-nine pence," I said. "And when you add in the money we made from the cake sale that would make it..."

I stopped to do the maths in my head.

"Two hundred and twenty-nine pounds and seventeen pence. That's almost enough to get my chair!"

"Actually, Doyin..."

I swung round. I hadn't seen Dad come into the room.

"Your mother and I have been talking," he said, nodding towards Mum. "As I said, you've made both of us very proud. So..."

He stopped and looked at Mum, who smiled.

"We'd like to give you something towards your chair, Doyin. How does fifty pounds sound?"

I couldn't believe it.

"It ... it sounds fantastic," I said. Then I felt a pang of guilt. "Are you sure you can afford it?"

Mum gave me a warm look and a big smile. "Dad and I have been doing extra shifts at work," she said. "We know how much this means to you."

"Wow! This is awesome. Thank you so much, Mum. Thanks, Dad. That means I've got more than enough for the deposit."

"Yes," said Mum. "But there's more. Coach Carlos knows everything you've been doing to raise money and ... well, why don't you tell him, Bola?"

"He's done some work with a charity called Whizz-Kidz," Dad said. "They've helped a couple of players in his team before. So he asked them if they could help you and they said yes."

"So ... what does that mean?" I asked, my heart pounding.

"They're going to pay for the rest of your chair," Dad told me.

"Bu t... but ... but..." I stammered. "I thought you said we didn't accept charity."

"I never said that!" Dad exclaimed. "Do you remember me saying anything like that, Christianah?"

"Those words never left your lips," said Mum, smiling broadly and knowingly, and giving me a wink.

I must have been in shock. I didn't know what to say or do.

"Hahh!!" Dad said. "So do we not at least get a hug from our soon-to-be-best-basketballer-in-Britain son?"

I giggled as I hugged them. They squeezed

me tight in their arms. For the first time in weeks, I felt completely happy. I didn't need to hide who I was, or what was going on. Everything was out in the open and it was all going to be okay.

"Mum, Dad..."

"Yes, what is it, Doyin?" they said together.

"This is the best day of my life."

Mum wiped a tear from her eye. I think I might even have spotted one or two in Dad's eyes.

"So you now have enough for your chair," Mum said, smiling at Dad and me, "and even a little extra to take your friends out for a slap-up meal. We think they deserve it."

"They do," I said. "But actually, if it's okay with you, Mum – and with you, Dad – there's something else I'd like to spend some of the extra money on. Something really important."

18
Project Projector

"**THANK YOU** Mr Jenkins, for that very interesting talk. I must say, I never knew that the majority of marine molluscs subsist on plant matter dissolved in water, which they ingest by filter feeding. Fascinating, absolutely fascinating."

Somewhere amongst the snoring and occasional belch in the audience there was a slightly less than enthusiastic round of applause.

"Now, to finish today's assembly we

have something of a mystery," Mrs Bolton continued. "A last-minute addition, a presentation by Ade Adepitan and some of his friends. They'll have to go some way to beat Mr Jenkins' extraordinary description of molluscs, but I'm sure it will be very entertaining. Mr Adepitan, over to you."

I was nervous as I made my way to the front of the hall. I'd never spoken in front of so many people before. The whole school was there, but everyone clapped and cheered (apart from Spencer and his mates, of course), and that made me feel a little better.

"Erm, th-thank you, Mrs ... er... Mrs B-Bolton."

It wasn't the greatest of starts. If I carried on like this, people would be booing and chucking tomatoes at me.

I shut my eyes for a moment and tried to connect with my powers. Cyborg Cat would help me deliver the perfect speech.

I braced myself, expecting the usual surge of energy to pass through my body.

Nothing happened.

I swallowed hard and gulped. My powers had stopped working at the worst possible moment.

"Don't just stand there like a lemon, get on with it, you loser!"

No prizes for guessing whose voice that was. I opened my eyes.

"Neville Spencer Frogley, be quiet right now or you'll be in detention for a week!"

Spencer turned red with embarrassment. Mrs Bolton had used his first name, Neville, which he detested. Fortunately, his outburst had given me just enough time to compose myself. I was going to have to do the presentation without the help of my powers.

I took a quick look over my shoulder. Brian, Dexter and Shed were waiting backstage to do their bit. Shed was giving me a 'Come on, you can do this' look. Brian was also giving me an encouraging look, but I think that was more because he wanted me to get on with it so he could do his part and show off a bit. I'm not sure Dexter had any idea what was really going on, but he was always positive and upbeat. They all gave me a thumbs up.

Melody and Emily were in the audience. Melody looked worried; she wasn't entirely sure what was going on. Emily locked eyes with me and I felt a bit of a jolt. Even though I couldn't seem to summon my Cyborg Cat powers, it felt good to know that my friends were with me.

I was about to start when something caught the corner of my eye. In the wings of the stage Dexter had stuck his tongue out and was doing a mad little dance. I laughed and my nerves evaporated.

"A little while ago," I said confidently, "something incredible happened to me. An injustice was brought to light. A criminal was caught."

There was a collective gasp from the audience.

"I didn't catch the criminal alone," I went on, "because my friends helped me. And one of them helped by doing something absolutely amazing. Didn't you, Melody Louise Watson?"

Melody almost jumped out of her seat. She had no idea about the speech, or our plan, or any of this.

"And —" I went on before she could answer — "it was caught on camera by the great director Brian 'The Brain' Kingston."

Brian had asked me to call him 'The Brain'. He said every director needed a catchy nickname.

"I've just come into some money, so I have

been able to buy a projector and screen, and I can show you exactly how Melody Watson helped catch a criminal who had been guilty of taking sponsorship money, money that was meant for a new sports wheelchair for me. Ready, lads?"

"Ready," came Shed's voice from behind the stage.

"Yeah, ready," said Dexter, who was also backstage.

That was their cue to bring out the screen. Unfortunately, instead of a slick, silent operation, everyone in the hall heard this.

"No, Dexter, you're meant to lift up the other end."

"But I'm already holding on to this end, Shed."

"So am I."

"Well, why don't you let go?"

"Why don't you let go?"

"Fine!"

"Ow! My foot!"

A moment later, Shed and Dexter appeared carrying the screen and, incredibly, managed to put it up without any more problems.

Brian had set up his projector. Now all I could do was pray that he had managed to connect his video camera up to the projector correctly.

"I think we're ready now," I said to the restless audience. "As I said, what you're going to see is truly amazing. Take it away, Brian."

"Thank you, Ade," Brian said, before pausing for dramatic effect. He was enjoying this moment a little too much. "Ladies and gentlemen of Credon Road School. The astounding, astonishing images you're about to witness were filmed on a JVC VHS-C compact camcorder by a highly proficient camera operator. As I'm sure you know, the

JVC VHS-C films on magnetic tape, which is wound on one main spool and –"

"Brian," I interrupted. "Could you just press 'play', like we arranged?"

"Well, Ade, I thought everyone would like to know a little –"

"Brian!" snapped Mrs Bolton. "I'm sure we'd all love to hear about your video camera, but assembly is due to finish in two minutes, so perhaps you could save it for another time?"

"Yes, Mrs Bolton," said Brian, and then, finally, he pressed play. The Parsons Road Street Party appeared on screen.

To be fair to Brian, he'd done a pretty good job. At first there was just general footage of the party, and some stuff with us all mucking about on camera, serving on the cake stall. Soon enough the film showed the balloons, and the chaos that ensued after the masks had crashed to the ground.

Brian had captured me spotting the Masked Marauder and giving chase, and everything that had happened until we thought we'd lost him.

Then it was Melody's big moment. As I looked at the audience, I could tell everyone was on the edge of their seats.

Brian had focused on the ball, but he expertly widened the shot out when Melody approached, so that you could see her properly.

In the distance you could just make out the Masked Marauder by the tree.

On screen, Melody kicked the

ball. Her foot struck, the ball curved round the tree and whacked into the Masked Marauder.

It looked even more impressive a banana shot on camera than it had in real life, if that was possible. I didn't think I could ever get bored of watching it. Melody had played an absolute blinder.

The hall erupted into cheers, claps, whistles and hoots. It was pandemonium.

They even started to chant Melody's name.

"MEL-O-DY! MEL-O-DY! MEL-O-DY!"

It took Mrs Bolton a good few seconds to calm everything down again.

"Well, thank you for that, Mr Adepitan," she said. "It really was quite something. And Melody, I have just been given a message for you from Mr Carmichael. He'd like you to report for football training on Thursday. Congratulations on becoming the first girl on the Credon Road team."

Melody beamed. We all did. Spencer and his mates were seething, but we didn't care about that.

"Hey, Ade..."

I turned to see Brian pointing the video camera at me.

"So how does it feel to be a superhero?"

"It feels great," I said, looking down at my chair, which had started to flicker mischievously. A bolt of energy flowed through me. I tried not to react, and gave Brian a wry smile as I continued, trying to sound mysterious. "But it's fraught with danger and excitement. Who knows what lies round the corner?"

"I do," said Dexter, popping up behind me. "It's the gym. It's just down the hallway and round the corner."

"No, you silly sausage, I meant –"

Dexter knew what I meant. He was smiling at me along with all the others.

I smiled too, but actually I'd really meant it. Another nemesis had been defeated, but there'd be more, of that I was certain.

I didn't know where or when the next threat would show up, but when it did one thing was for certain. Cyborg Cat and the Parsons Road Gang would be ready.

Cat-like reflexes, super skills ...You've never met a superhero who rolls like this!

The

series

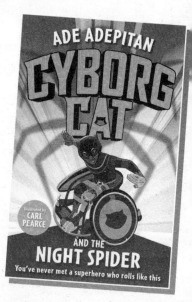

Available in all places good books are sold